A VERY QUIET PLACE

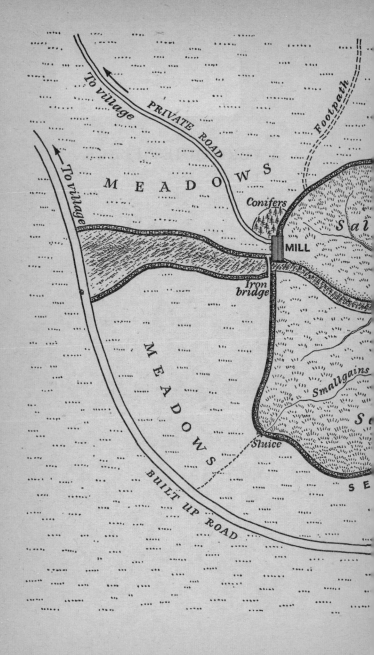

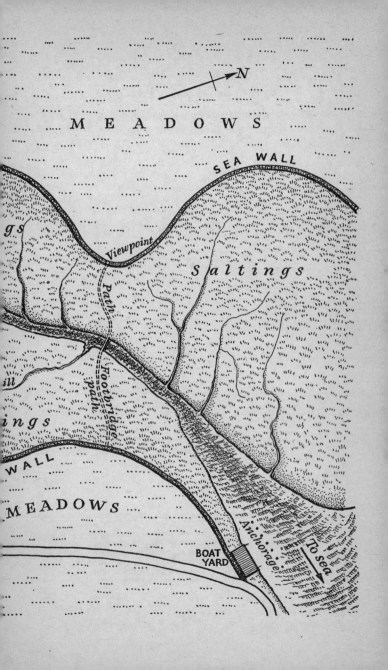

By the same author in PAN Books

THE HOUSE OF SOLDIERS

THE ASHES OF LODA

ANDREW GARVE

A VERY QUIET PLACE

UNABRIDGED

PAN BOOKS LTD : LONDON

First published 1967 by William Collins Sons & Co. Ltd.

This edition published 1968 by Pan Books Ltd.,
33 Tothill Street, London, S.W.1

330 02187 7

Printed in Great Britain by
Richard Clay (The Chaucer Press), Ltd.,
Bungay, Suffolk

ONE

Chapter One

THE LIGHTS in the little studio behind Regent Street were still burning at ten o'clock on that Friday evening. Debbie Sheldon was working later than usual. Several new jobs had come in during the week – and as a free-lance in the hard, competitive world of commercial photography, she hadn't dared to turn any of them down. The busy times made up for the others, when work was scarce. Hence the overtime . . .

Debbie was twenty-five years old. Men of all ages thought her attractive, and even women didn't find much to criticize. She had dark brown hair which she allowed to fall smoothly to her shoulders during working hours, big brown eyes with long curling lashes, and a smile that met you more than halfway. She was five feet three inches tall, with everything nicely distributed. On this busy September evening she was wearing her usual studio garb of navy blue and white striped cotton sweater, slim-fitting navy blue slacks, and almost invisible sandals on bare feet. It was a workmanlike outfit in which she looked unmistakably feminine.

Debbie had set up in business as a commercial photographer in a small way just twelve months before. After five years in the creative department of Harley and Swain, the big advertising firm, she'd felt technically equipped to work on her own, and when an opportunity had come she'd taken the risk and rented this back-lane studio with an adjoining bed-sitter. The first few months had been a desperate struggle – but now the worst seemed to be over. Debbie had proved to have the right qualities for a free-lance. She'd been able to exploit a rather special aptitude – an eye for the arrangement and lighting of small, inanimate objects, a feeling for shape and texture, which gave individuality to her work – and she'd shown a marked flair for the advertising angle. Her conscientiousness, and the fact that she was a cheerful, friendly person to deal with had also helped in the building of her business. Clients liked her, as well as her work, and they usually came back for more.

She was busy now, at the tail end of the day, experimenting with a new subject which she intended to photograph next morning – a place setting of Minton china and wineglasses, with an elaborate branched candlestick in the background. As usual, she was seeking an elusive perfection. She tried numerous arrangements, adjusting the china, advancing the candlestick, shifting the various wineglasses a millimetre this way or that, testing out various backgrounds and lighting positions. Intent and absorbed, she moved around the table like a high priestess engaged in some arcane ritual. It was well after eleven before she felt reasonably satisfied with the effect she'd achieved. Then, leaving everything ready for an early start next day, she went into the sitting-room to unwind with a cigarette before bed.

It was a small room for all the purposes it had to serve, but Debbie was an expert in the art of economizing space and she was proud of the way she'd arranged things. She'd had built-in cupboards put up in every suitable place, rather on the lines of a ship's cabin, so that she could store away all the paraphernalia of a busy and varied life and still keep the room looking neat and uncluttered as she preferred it. She'd made a tailored cover of black linen for her divan bed, and for daytime use its pillows were transformed into gaily-coloured cushions. There was a narrow rosewood table with a deep hanging flap which could be raised when necessary and which also served to conceal the black stools that she used as dining chairs when she was entertaining. Like the studio, the room was painted white, and it had an overall carpet in her favourite sludge green colour. There was just one picture – a brilliant lithograph of Chinese ducks – and opposite it a beautiful little Regency looking-glass which she hadn't been able to resist buying, although she knew it had been a gross extravagance.

As she looked appraisingly round, she couldn't help recalling the rather sordid appearance of the place when she'd moved into it just over a year ago. Of course, there was a lot more to be done yet – if she could ever take the time off to do it. A cunning arrangement of combined bedhead and bookshelves would be useful ... And the second-hand armchair must be re-covered. It looked more modern since she'd had the legs sawn off – but what she really wanted was a super-luxury one in black leather, preferably on a swivel. Well, all in good time ...

Presently she switched her attention to a new camera that had arrived only that day. It was a Diplex 204 automatic, with a very powerful rotating flash cube that gave four flashes without having to be changed. Again, it was a bit of an extravagance, because she didn't do much flash work in the studio – but she liked to have the tools ready for any job, just as she liked to have the clothes for any occasion. And it would certainly be a lovely plaything. She read the instructions, tried the viewfinder, examined the automatic loading, put in the first film. It was a small camera, a beautiful precision instrument, and very handy to carry about. It would be just the thing to take on a holiday, when she could afford one ... Pleased with her purchase, she placed it carefully on top of a tallboy so that she could admire it as she undressed.

At some point in the night, she woke with a start. A noise had roused her – she didn't know what. She lay listening in the darkness. She could hear a car engine running in the street below. Perhaps that was what had disturbed her. Then the venetian blind over the window gave a loud rattle and she felt cool air on her face. Of course – the blind. It always vibrated when the wind got up. She switched on the wall light over her head, looked at her watch, and made a face. Five minutes past four. A bad time to wake. She'd probably have to lie and read now for a bit. She got out of bed to shut the window.

As she glanced down through the angled slats of the blind, she saw the car she had heard. It was a large black one, parked directly opposite her on the other side of the narrow lane. A man was sitting at the wheel. He kept looking around and behind him, as though he was nervous. Another man was getting out of the car. He approached a door and tapped on it, and the door opened.

Debbie stood gaping. The door, she knew, was the side entrance to Anstey's the jewellers. She couldn't believe that the men could have honest business there at four o'clock in the morning. They certainly didn't look honest – they were behaving most furtively. Perhaps she ought to tell somebody. Ring the police. She crossed to the telephone and dialled 999. A woman's voice said, 'Emergency – what service do you...?' Debbie cut in breathlessly. 'There's something going on at Anstey's in Regent Street ... A man's just gone in through the Lever Lane door and there's a black car waiting outside...' Then, as she heard the engine revving up, she dropped the receiver on its rest and darted back to the window. Three men were coming out of the side door. One of them was carrying a suitcase. They were getting into the car. On a sudden impulse, Debbie grabbed the camera from the top of the tallboy, thrust it under the blind, and pressed the trigger. As the flash bulb went off, the car roared away.

To Debbie, who had never dialled 999 before, the effect of her call was staggering. In a matter of seconds, it seemed, the lane was blocked by police cars. With a minimum of noise and excitement, dark figures began inspecting doors and grilles by the light of torches. Someone in authority was giving quiet instructions. In a few minutes a man appeared with a ladder and another man climbed to an upper window and somehow got through. Presently the side door opened and most of the policemen trooped in. The door closed behind them. For the moment, that seemed to be all.

Debbie stood uncertainly, wondering what she'd better

do. She hadn't the least desire to become more involved in the affair than she already was, but she supposed the police would want all the information they could get and she was in a special position to help them. Except for her own flat, the four-storey building where she lived consisted entirely of offices, empty at night, so she was almost certainly the only witness of what had happened. But she couldn't tell them much more at the moment than she had done. Nothing really useful, until the photograph was developed. Perhaps not even then – but there was a chance. The first thing was to see what she'd got on the film. She put on a dressing-gown and took the camera into the dark-room that opened out of the studio.

She felt a stir of excitement as the first shadow appeared under the developer and the vague shape of a car slowly emerged. At least she'd pointed the thing in the right direction. But with a camera she'd never used before, she might easily have made a mess of the picture. In the glow of the red lamp she watched the clock. Half a minute to go. There ... Now for the fixing tank ... She waited, with unprofessional impatience.

When, finally, she held the negative to the light, she saw that it was almost perfect. The flash had given excellent illumination, thanks to the narrowness of the street. The focus was sharp, and there was good detail in the face of the car driver. The negative should print well. Debbie switched on the fan-heater in the dark-room and pegged the film up to dry.

She went back to the window. It was almost daylight now. The police cars had been joined by others, some of them with 'Press' stickers on their windscreens. A group of men who looked as though they might be reporters were talking to an officer on the corner. A few sightseers had gathered there, too. Otherwise, the street was still remarkably quiet. Debbie went into the little cubby-hole she'd fitted out as a kitchen and brewed herself some tea. While she was drinking it she heard an ambulance bell. She crossed to the window again and looked out. The ambulance was just turning into Lever Lane. It pulled up near the side door of the jewellers. She watched two men go in with a stretcher. Almost at once they reappeared. This time there was a humped shape on the stretcher, with a blanket completely over it. The sight shook Debbie. Until now, the episode of the night had seemed a small adventure, slightly stimulating, not quite believable. Shadowy robbers slipping away in the dark . . . Now it seemed horrible, and very real.

She bathed and dressed, and made coffee and toast, while the film dried. By the time she'd finished breakfast it was ready for printing. Back in the dark-room, she made a single positive, fixed it, and brought it to the light. The promise of the negative had been fulfilled. Three men in the car were no more than dim shapes behind the glass, but the fourth, the driver, had been caught with his window down and almost full face, as though he'd been looking up at the flat. He had a very large, asymmetrical nose and close-set eyes. Debbie, studying his features under a magnifying glass, felt she would recognize him at once if she saw him again. The photo would have to be enlarged, but the police could do that . . . Now – should she take the picture down and give it to one of the officers outside, or should she dial 999 again and say she'd got it?

The question was suddenly answered for her. The telephone rang. As she picked up the receiver a brisk voice said, 'This is Scotland Yard – Superintendent Jenkins. Who am I speaking to, please?'

Debbie told him.

'Miss Sheldon, an emergency telephone call was made at four o'clock this morning, and it's been traced to your number. It reported suspicious movements at Anstey's the jewellers. Did you make it?'

'Yes,' Debbie said.

'Ah . . . You should always give your name, you know, when you dial 999 with information – not just hang up. It would have saved us a lot of trouble.'

'I'm sorry,' Debbie said. 'I wanted to get back to the window and see what was happening.'

'What *was* happening? Can you describe any of the men?'

'I can do better than that,' Debbie said. 'I took a photograph of them. A flashlight.'

'You did?' The superintendent suddenly sounded much friendlier. 'Well, that could be a bit of luck. I'll send someone round for it right away and we'll get it developed.'

'I've developed it,' Debbie said. 'I've got a print all ready for you. It's my job – I'm a photographer.'

'I see . . . How well has the picture come out?'

'It's very good indeed of the driver of the car.'

'Splendid . . .! All right, Miss Sheldon – one of our sergeants will be calling for the picture in about half an hour. Sergeant Macey . . . And later on I shall want to hear your full story. Would you mind staying near the telephone?'

'I'll do that, of course,' Debbie said.

'Good – I'll be ringing you back. In the meantime, I think you'd be wise not to talk to anyone about what you saw.'

'I won't say a word.'

'Fine . . . Goodbye, then. And we're most grateful to you for the help you've given us.'

Debbie dried the print and put it in an envelope with the negative. Then, while she waited for Sergeant Macey to arrive, she washed up and went through the daily routine that made her living-room look quite unlike a bedroom – smoothing the black linen over the divan, zipping up the pillows in their bright covers, stowing slippers and dressing-gown in their appropriate places. When heavy footfalls sounded outside on the landing at around eight o'clock she presented herself at the door, conscious that everything was in apple-pie order behind her. But it wasn't the sergeant – it was a couple of men in overalls, climbing to the next floor. She suddenly remembered that the office above her was moving out that day.

The sounds of coming and going on the stairs grew

steadily in volume as the men got to work. There seemed to be four of them now. Odd snatches of remover's jargon reached Debbie's ears through the door – 'Cuddle it, Jimmy' – 'Pitch her a bit' – 'She's yours, Bill.' Once there was a thud against the wall as something slipped. Office workers arriving for Saturday duty added to the noise and congestion. Then, at last, there came a rap on the door. A dark, very spruce man of about thirty said, 'Miss Sheldon . . .? I'm Sergeant Macey.'

'Come in,' Debbie said. The sergeant followed her in and she closed the door.

'Thought I'd need a shoehorn to get me up those stairs,' Macey said, with a grin. 'Well, now – what about this picture?'

Debbie gave him the envelope. Macey glanced inside it, took out the print, and studied it. 'Yes – it's pretty good,' he said. 'Sort of familiar, too, that fellow's face. I wouldn't be surprised if we knew him.' He jerked his head across towards the window. 'A bad business that was, last night. They killed a man, you know.'

Debbie nodded. 'I saw the ambulance take him away . . . What happened?'

'They knocked him on the head – then they tied him up and gagged him. And he choked to death. He was a sort of caretaker – slept there at night. They must have crept up on him.'

'How ghastly . . .! Did they steal much?'

'They took pretty well everything that was worth taking . . .' Macey put the envelope carefully away in his breast pocket. 'Well, I'd better be pushing along – we'll want to get this picture circulated as soon as possible . . . You made just the one copy, did you?'

'That's all.'

'Oh, well, we can easily make some more . . . Right, Miss, many thanks. You'll be hearing from Superintendent Jenkins later.' Macey opened the door, waited for two removal men and an office desk to pass, and departed with a friendly smile.

Left to herself, Debbie stood by the window for a moment, her face clouding as she recalled the night scene and thought about the caretaker. How dreadful to be quietly getting one's meal, or reading the paper, or whatever caretakers did in the long night hours – and then suddenly have everything turn into violence and chaos ... She was glad she'd been able to take that photograph. It wouldn't help the poor man who'd died, but it would have been well worth while if it helped the police to track down the criminals ...

She turned away. She'd been relieved of all responsibility and there was nothing more she could do, so she'd better get on with her day's programme. She didn't at all mind staying indoors for the superintendent's call – a gusty wind was blowing outside and it had just started to rain. And there was nothing like work to take one's mind off unpleasant things.

She spent an active and a varied morning. First she checked the lighting and arrangement of the Minton china set, and took her photographs. She couldn't process them right away because there was no telephone in the dark-room and she daren't shut herself up – but she had a feeling they were going to be a success. With the professional work out of the way, she turned her attention to the household chores she usually reserved for the weekend – paying bills, doing her accounts, and making a list of non-urgent letters to be answered. At eleven-thirty she took a break for coffee and mentally reviewed her wardrobe. Red woollen coat to go to the cleaners ... At least two inches to come off the hem of last year's heavy coat ... And she must buy something really striking to wear at Sarah's wedding next month. Sarah Underwood had been in the creative department with her at Harley and Swain, but on the copy side, while Debbie had been in 'visual'. She'd been terribly envious when Debbie had taken the plunge into free-lance work – but now she was getting married she'd stopped lamenting. Her fiancé was in advertising, too – a charming young man; though Debbie wasn't sure she liked the smooth, sophisticated men who peopled that world. Not for marriage, anyway ... Now what were her engagements? She leafed through her diary for the next few days. Nothing social for today, thank goodness, but she'd promised to have coffee with Jennifer in the morning and go to a party at Nigel's on Sunday evening. On Monday there was the ceramic tile job to finish off, and lunch with her agent, and – heavens! – a cocktail party at Carol's. Never a dull moment...!

Several people telephoned during the morning – one of them Sarah, to whom Debbie would have loved to confide her night's story, but didn't. Another was a woman who wanted some passport photographs in a hurry. Debbie explained that she didn't do portraits, but suggested a place that might be open. It was an annoying interruption, because the one o'clock news had just started and she missed the item about the jewel robbery, which she'd wanted to hear.

It was well on into the afternoon when the superintendent phoned again. This time he was extremely affable.

'Sorry if I've kept you in, Miss Sheldon – I haven't had a moment until now.'

'That's quite all right,' Debbie said.

'This picture of yours – it's excellent. I think it's probably given us just the lead we needed. We've been able to trace the driver in our records – or a man very like him. If we're right, he goes under the name of Thomas Blake and he lives in Eastbourne. So you've done a splendid job for us, and we're most grateful.'

'Thank you,' Debbie said.

'Now the thing is this,' Jenkins went on. 'Wherever he was last night, Blake is back in Eastbourne now and we've got him under surveillance there. But we don't want to pick him up yet, because if he is our man and he doesn't know he's being watched there's a chance he'll lead us to the others. What we would like is for you to take a discreet look at him and confirm the identification. After all, you actually

16

saw him in the car. Do you think you could possibly go to Eastbourne this evening?'

'Well...' Debbie began.

'It's asking a lot, I know,' Jenkins said, 'but it is of the greatest importance. All you'll need is an overnight bag – we'll fix a reservation for you at the Grand Hotel, and you'll be able to come back first thing in the morning, and of course we'll see you're not out of pocket. If you agree, I'd like you to catch the seven-ten from Victoria. An officer of the Eastbourne CID – Inspector Crowley – will meet you with a car at Eastbourne station and take over from there. Sergeant Macey has given him a description of you and we've told him you'll carry a book under your arm as you leave the platform. I do hope we can count on you, Miss Sheldon. It may make all the difference to catching this gang.'

'Yes, I see,' Debbie said. 'Well, I don't seem to have much choice, do I?'

The prospect of a ninety-minute train journey and a wet evening in Eastbourne wasn't exactly inspiring, but having agreed to go Debbie decided to make the best of it. Helping the police could be quite an interesting experience, she told herself – and a night at the Grand Hotel shouldn't be too bad. She rang Jennifer to postpone their morning date, packed a sophisticated little dark dress and a pair of smart shoes, as well as her night things, slipped a book into her case, and at six-thirty phoned for a taxi.

She reached Victoria in a downpour of rain, bought her ticket and an *Evening Standard*, and made her way to the train, which was a non-stop to Eastbourne. The coaches were sparsely occupied, and she soon found an empty compartment. She settled down in a corner seat by the far door, away from the corridor, and opened her paper.

She'd barely had time to glance at the huge headline – WEST END JEWEL GRAB WATCHMAN KILLED – when a woman entered with a good deal of fuss and took a corner seat by the corridor. She was well-dressed, middle-aged – and voluble. She began to talk, first about the weather, which Debbie agreed was atrocious, and then about a matinée she'd been to that afternoon. It was a play that Debbie herself had seen and liked, and she was quite happy to discuss it for a while. Then the woman went on to talk about herself, her husband, her dog, and a holiday she'd just had in Madeira. It wasn't until the train was well out into Surrey that the flow dried up and Debbie could turn again to her paper.

Now, for the first time, she was able to read what had actually happened at Anstey's. The story ran:

A night watchman was killed and jewellery worth more than half a million pounds was stolen when thieves raided Anstey's in Regent Street last night.

The watchman was Mr Tom Shaw, 63, of Crane Avenue, Islington. He had been brutally coshed, tied up, and gagged. Death resulted from suffocation caused by the gag.

The alarm was raised at four o'clock this morning by a woman who telephoned the police anonymously and reported suspicious movements outside the shop.

It appears that the robbers entered the premises late yesterday evening, using keys to a side door. This, and the intimate knowledge they showed of the layout of the place, suggests that they had received inside help at some time.

One of the gang dealt expertly with the intricate burglar alarm system, fixing it in such a way that the secret circuit remained intact and the link to Scotland Yard's information room was broken. The strong room was blown with gelignite in an equally expert fashion.

The jewellery, much of it deposited by wealthy clients for safe-keeping during the holiday season, was selectively taken. The haul included emerald and diamond earrings, diamond and sapphire brooches, tiaras, pearls, rubies, and gold. Many of the pieces are distinctive, but the settings are likely to be destroyed, the diamonds re-cut and the gold melted down.

From the techniques employed, the police think it probable that the gang was the same one that broke into Fawley's in Victoria Street, last May. On that occasion, also, a caretaker was murdered. The haul then was only £20,000, as a result of a stock switch to another branch on the day of the robbery.

Detectives were today seeking underworld informants who might give them a lead to the Anstey robbers. So far they have little to go on. A black Ford Zephyr car, believed to have been used by the gang for their getaway, was found abandoned early this morning in Archer Street, a quarter of a mile away. It had been stolen, and afforded no clue to the robbers.

Debbie looked up as a ticket inspector came in. The woman in the far corner, who was dozing, had to be gently nudged awake. Debbie showed her ticket. As the inspector left, another man passing along the corridor paused at the door, caught Debbie's eye, and gave her a long, hard stare.

A gust of rain lashed the windows. Dusk was beginning to fall. The drenched countryside looked most uninviting. Debbie returned to her paper, and the rest of the robbery story. There was one more paragraph.

A Scotland Yard spokesman said this afternoon, 'We are dealing here with an exceptionally dangerous gang. The callous treatment of the watchman, who was left to die while the robbery was completed, indicates a total disregard for human life. We repeat our urgent appeal to the anonymous woman caller to come forward and help the police with their inquiries.'

Debbie frowned. That was odd ... Scotland Yard had known by eight o'clock in the morning who the anonymous caller was. Nearly twelve hours ago. So why were they still appealing? The paper must have made a mistake ... Yet the sentence could hardly have been more specific. She stared at the words 'this afternoon' and 'repeat' ... Perhaps there'd been some failure of liaison at Scotland Yard. Perhaps that was the explanation. All the same ...

Her thoughts went back to the first call Superintendent Jenkins had made, and what he'd said. Naturally she hadn't questioned anything at the time. But now ... With dismay, she remembered a conversation she'd had with Sarah a few weeks ago. Some pest had been making unpleasant phone calls, and the police had told Sarah that the only thing to do was to keep him talking and get someone else to ring them on another line, because a dialled call couldn't be traced once the caller had hung up ... So how had the police traced the call *she'd* made?

Alarm bells were ringing loudly now. As Debbie looked back over the events of the day, her doubts increased to near-certainty. She didn't know much about these things – but surely, once the police had discovered she'd been a witness of the robbery, they'd have wanted to see her right away and hear everything she could tell them. They'd have wanted to make sure of her evidence. They'd never have left her alone all day without asking a single question. She simply didn't believe it.

Her mouth grew dry. The conclusion was inescapable – and very frightening. It *hadn't* been the police she'd been talking to. It hadn't been the police who'd collected the photograph. Someone else had collected it.... And who would have wanted it, who would have *known* about it, except a member of the gang...? Those men in the car must have realized they'd been photographed when the flash went off. Somehow – though Debbie couldn't imagine how – they'd found out about her. They'd rung up and checked on her, and then one of them had called and taken the picture away. The negative too – he hadn't even had to ask for it. All the evidence ...

And there was worse to come. She was on her way to meet one of them! That story about wanting her to identify a man under surveillance must have been phoney, too. They'd invented it to get her out into the country. She was going to be picked up by one of them in a car – and he was going to take her to a quiet spot and get rid of her. She hadn't a doubt of it. She'd seen the photograph, she could describe the driver of the car – and these men were killers. She was going straight into a trap – on a non-stop train!

She sat rigid with fear, her heart thumping wildly. She knew she must do something – but what...? Wake the woman opposite and tell her? Go and find some reliable male passenger and ask for protection? Look for the guard? Find a policeman at Eastbourne...? What about that man who'd stared in – had he been watching her? She felt horribly exposed. Whatever she did, a gang as desperate as this one must be would hardly let her get away...

She didn't notice that the train was braking until it had actually stopped. She looked out of the rain-soaked window. She could just make out a platform – but the station was in darkness and she couldn't read the name. She let the window down and leaned out. A red light turned to green at the end of the platform and the train began to move again...

Debbie grabbed her handbag and suitcase and opened the door. The train still hadn't gathered much speed. She heard the dozing woman stir and murmur something. She leapt out on to the platform, stumbled, nearly fell, recovered herself. She saw the woman's arm, feeling for the door to slam it shut. She saw the woman's face, staring after her. The carriages went by. Slowly, the rear light of the train receded into the distance – and Debbie was left alone.

She drew a long breath of relief. The rain was bucketing down, but she didn't care. She'd no idea where she was, but she didn't care about that, either. She'd got away – clean away. That was all that mattered. She would walk until she came to a telephone, and ring for a taxi to come and pick her up at the box. She couldn't be far from Eastbourne – the train was due there in a few minutes. It shouldn't be difficult to get someone to come out.

She peered at a name plate on a seat. She couldn't read it

in the dark. She fumbled damply for her lighter, flicked it on and read the name as the flame blew out. Pole Halt. Probably it was one of those little-used stations that closed early for the night. It was certainly closed now. Not a light showed anywhere. The wooden ticket office was firmly shut. So was the exit. Debbie walked to the end of the platform and found an unlocked gate by a crossover and went through it into the station approach.

The road that ran past the station was no more than a narrow lane. There were no houses in sight, no sign of life at all. Debbie could tell by the scents and the silence and the loom of the trees that she was in deep country. It might be quite a way to a phone box. She debated whether to turn to the left or the right, and chose the left. The lane appeared to be flanked by thick, scrubby woodland. It was a black and lonely place – but compared with the train, it felt secure. She started walking, head down to the wind, thankful that her suitcase was no heavier.

The feeling of security didn't last long. She hadn't gone more than a few yards before she began thinking about the man who was waiting for her in the car at Eastbourne. What would he do now? He probably knew that she'd caught the train. He'd know it was a non-stop train. When she didn't get out at the terminus he'd wonder what had happened to her. He'd probably find out that the train had stopped at Pole Halt. He'd know she *must* have got out there.

Suppose he came to look for her? It was only a few miles – and on this road, he couldn't miss her ... Fear gripped her again. She quickened her step ...

Chapter Two

HUGH FREEMAN drove along the lane at a fast pace, throwing up waves of mud and water from his wheels. It was no night to be out in an ancient car with a canvas hood and no side screens and he was eager to get home.

The windscreen wiper was giving a bit of trouble and visibility through the streaming glass was poor, but Hugh kept cracking along quite happily. He'd never yet met anything in this lane at night – and he knew every bend and every pothole. All around here was his home ground – the woods on the right, with the line of Downs behind them; the rough scrub on the left, screening the big, worked-out quarry and the grassy bank above it where he'd spent many a pleasant summer afternoon. Familiar, friendly country ...

He negotiated a corner – then suddenly braked as something showed in his headlights. A walking figure. A girl, lugging a suitcase. Now where on earth could she be going ...? As the lights caught her she looked round sharply, stopped, and shrank back into the roadside. Her face was pale and strained, her eyes enormous. Hugh slowed right down. She made no signal, but he couldn't believe she wanted to go on hiking in the pouring rain. She must be soaked to the skin. He pulled up beside her and stuck his head out. 'Can I give you a lift?' he said.

The girl didn't answer. Instead, incredibly, she dropped her suitcase and dived into the undergrowth like a frightened animal.

For a moment, Hugh just gaped after her. He could understand a girl not wanting to accept a lift from a strange man in a lonely lane, but this was going a bit far. He pulled the car in to the side of the road, wondering what to do about her. He could hear the sound of breaking twigs, of a panic struggle through the bushes. She could easily hurt herself... Suddenly he remembered the quarry...

He shot out of the car and plunged in after her. 'Be careful!' he shouted. 'There's a big drop there...' A tree branch lashed his face and brambles tore at his legs. He could hardly see a thing, but he could still hear the girl, not far ahead. He shouted his warning again and fought his way on, his hands outstretched to ward off obstructions. Somewhere here, he remembered, there was a wooden hut. It loomed up, right ahead of him, and he swung to the left and went round it and came out on the grassy bank. Now it was only a few yards to the edge of the quarry. The girl was just in front of him, a patch of blacker darkness in the dark. He hurled himself forward and grabbed her, and she gave a terrified scream.

He clamped a hand over her mouth and held her struggling body tight while he spoke into her ear. 'Easy, now!' he said. 'There's nothing to be afraid of. I'm not going to hurt you. You could have broken your neck. Look...!' He pointed ahead, and down. Far below, fifty feet below, there was the faint glint of water. 'It's a quarry,' he said. 'Didn't you hear me call?'

Debbie looked down. Hugh felt her body relax in his grasp and draw back, away from the edge. He released her. 'What on earth did you rush off like that for?' he asked. 'I'm a perfectly ordinary, harmless chap...'

She couldn't see his face – but his voice was gentle, reassuring. He didn't sound like a gangster. And he *had* stopped her going over the edge – so he must be all right. She'd let her fears run away with her.

'I'm sorry,' she said shakily. 'I thought you were following me. I thought you were the man who...' She broke off. 'It's such a long story...'

Hugh said, 'Let's get out of the rain.' He drew her into the comparative shelter of the wooden hut. It was open-fronted, a rough protection for some stacks of logs. 'Now, what's the trouble? Who are you scared of?'

Debbie told him. It was a relief to tell someone, even a

stranger. She told him about the robbery, and the photograph, and the bogus policemen, and her appointment in Eastbourne, and her flight from the train, and her terror when the car had appeared in the lane. She didn't go into too many details – she just gave him an outline of what had happened. Even so, it took quite a time.

Hugh heard her out in silence. When she'd finished he said, 'It all sounds frightfully melodramatic... Are you sure you aren't making a mistake – imagining things? It probably *was* the police, you know.'

'I'm sure it wasn't.'

'Well, anyway, you're safe enough now,' he said. 'What do you want me to do? If you like I'll run you into Lewes – it's as near as Eastbourne, and you could get a train back to London from there.'

'It's terribly kind of you,' Debbie said. 'I'd like to go back – thank you very much ... I'm sorry I was such an idiot.'

'Not at all – you've had a scaring time... Look, hang on a minute and I'll fetch a torch from the car. There's no need to tear yourself to ribbons again.'

He turned and set off back through the dripping undergrowth. It was no more than thirty yards to the road and this time he took it slowly – but even so it was a painful passage. He emerged with a gouged forehead, collected his torch from the car, switched off the headlights, and started to retrace his steps.

He'd barely re-entered the wood when the headlights of another car swept the road. It was coming from the direction of the station, travelling fast. He wondered if he'd left enough room for it to pass. He paused, and watched. It slowed down, and seemed about to ease by – then it suddenly pulled in behind his own car, and stopped. He heard a voice say, 'Yes, it's her suitcase, all right.'

He switched off his torch and ducked down. Two men had got out of the car. They had torches, too. They were examining the girl's case, which was still lying by the roadside. After a moment they moved to Hugh's car. One of them said, 'Whoever owns this crate must be with her. What the hell are they up to?' The other said, 'Well, we'll have to find them – they can't be far away.' They walked back to their own car, and one of them took something from the back seat. As they passed again through their headlight beam, Hugh saw with a sense of outrage that they were both carrying iron bars. The girl hadn't been mistaken after all!

For a moment, he hesitated. The men were obviously going to search the wood. They might miss both himself and the girl – but, with their lights, the odds were that they wouldn't. The girl, unsuspecting, would probably give herself away when she heard movement. Flight seemed the best bet. Hugh scrambled up, flicked on his own torch, and started to batter his way back through the wood, ignoring the sudden outbreak of noise behind him. He was still well ahead when he reached the hut. He grabbed Debbie's arm. 'You were right,' he said, 'there are two men after you. Come on!'

Debbie needed no exhorting. She could see the two torches flashing through the trees. She felt horribly afraid again – but at least she wasn't alone now. And the man with her was comfortingly large and strong. She could still feel his bear-hug. She started to run, side by side with him, guided by his torch. Along the grassy bank, well away from the quarry edge.

As they ran, Hugh tried to work out the best escape route. There was little hope of eluding the men on this side of the quarry. A hundred yards ahead, he recalled, the bank narrowed to a few feet. It would be dangerous for running – and it gave no cover. They must get over to the other side. Somewhere to the right, he remembered, there was a path leading down to the quarry bottom. Across the quarry, at its northern end, there was a big patch of gorse, cut by innumerable tracks. One of the tracks came out on a lane. If they could reach the gorse, they'd have a good chance. The pursuers, without local knowledge, would probably get lost in the tangle. It should be possible to throw them off there.

The sloping path suddenly showed up in the torch beam. 'Down the hill!' Hugh cried. Debbie swerved without slowing, and they raced on. In a few moments they were out on the level floor of the quarry. Hugh glanced over his shoulder. The pursuing torches were nearer. The men had followed down the path and were only twenty yards behind. 'They're catching us up,' Hugh said. 'Can you go faster?' Debbie put on a spurt – but she knew it couldn't last. She was finding it hard enough to keep up as it was. The pace was too hot for her. Her legs weren't long enough – and she had the wrong shoes on for running . . .

Hugh took her arm and helped her, half lifting and half dragging her. 'Keep going!' he urged her. 'You've *got* to keep going . . .' He steered her along the edge of a shallow pool and across to the other side of the quarry. She was running better now, drawn on by the strong pull of his arm, driven on by the pounding feet behind . . . Then, as the firm earth floor changed to crunching gravel, disaster hit them. Suddenly, Debbie stumbled. 'My shoe . . . !' she cried. It had gone – and there was no hope of recovering it. The pursuers were audibly closing the gap. She shook off the other shoe and tried to carry on. The gravel was agony under her feet. Fear was robbing her of breath. She'd never make it now. 'I can't,' she moaned. 'I can't . . .'

Hugh swung her towards the quarry face in a last, desperate manoeuvre. 'Listen,' he said, 'there are some breaks in the wall along here . . . Places where the water's run down . . . When we see one I'll switch the torch off . . . You throw yourself into it and lie still . . . I'll go on . . . I'll come back for you . . . Okay?'

'Yes,' Debbie gasped.

They moved close to the wall and ran parallel with it. Hugh's torch, pointing ahead, illuminated the indented edge. A line of shadow marked the first break. '*There!*' he said. 'See . . .?' They drew level with it. Hugh switched the light off and gave the girl a hard push. Immediately he swerved to the right, stamping his feet down on the gravel, noisily scraping and stumbling, momentarily flicking the light on and off to show his position. The seconds that followed were the worst of his life. If the men had guessed ... He glanced back. They were still coming on. The trick had worked. And now they wouldn't catch him. He'd plenty of strength left and he'd got their measure. He ran on beside the wall, still on gravel, holding the gap. Once he cried, 'I think we'll make it!' as though the girl were still with him. He rounded the head of another pool, put on speed, switched the torch on and off once more, doubled to the left, and found himself on grass. His footsteps were now muted. A track opened up between gorse bushes and he dived in among them and flung himself down, panting, watching the torches of the men. For a while they continued to move forward, well beyond the point where he'd doubled. Then the lights became stationary. They were about a hundred yards away. The men were talking. Hugh could hear their voices, but not what they were saying. They were still on gravel. They began to move around in widening circles, shining their torches on the ground. Looking for footmarks, Hugh thought. They searched for ten minutes and came together again. Their voices were louder now – they seemed to be arguing. Presently they moved off to the right, in the direction of the cars. The gravel had beaten them. They'd given up ...

Hugh waited, watching the lights recede. The men were going back under the opposite wall. They were the full width of the quarry away. They were making for the sloping path. They were climbing it ... In a moment, the lights had disappeared among the trees.

Hugh raised himself from the squelching ground. Slowly, stiffly, he began to make his way back along the top of the quarry wall in search of the girl. At intervals of a few yards he stopped and called down – 'Are you there?' He called four times before the girl answered. Then he lowered himself cautiously down the eroded watercourse and joined her.

'They've gone,' he said.

'Yes, I saw...'

'Are you all right?'

'More or less,' Debbie said. She was soaked to the skin, caked with mud and scratched with brambles; her stockings were torn to shreds, she was barefoot, and she felt bruised all over from her fall on the gravel – but she was very far from complaining. She was alive, which was more than she'd expected to be. 'Do you think there's any chance of finding my shoes?'

'I don't think it would be safe to look,' Hugh said. 'They're sure to be watching for a light – and we don't want them back here.'

'What are we going to do?'

'Well, we shan't be able to use the car again tonight, that's a certainty ... Look, I live only a mile and a half from here. Do you think you can make it?'

'I'll try.'

'All right – let's go....' Hugh took the girl's arm and helped her up the watercourse. At the top of the wall he turned to the right, back towards the gorse bushes, looking for the track that led to the lane. Presently he found it. The rain, which had stopped for a while, was coming on again. Debbie was limping badly. At each step, the limp grew worse.

'I'd better carry you,' Hugh said.

'Can you? All that way?'

'I expect so ... How would you like it – fireman's lift or pick-a-back?'

'I don't mind,' Debbie said.

Hugh bent down, put an arm round her legs, and raised her easily over his shoulder. 'How's that?'

'Very comfortable...' She felt so tired, she could have fallen asleep there and then, except that her head kept jerking when he started to walk.

'What's that banging against me?'

'Sorry – it's my handbag.'

'Good lord, have you still got that?'

'Of course...'

They didn't talk any more. There were some uphill bits, once they reached the lane, and Hugh needed all his breath. They met no one and saw nothing. After thirty slogging minutes through dark and empty country, a white gate gleamed.

'Here we are ...' Hugh unlatched the gate, continued along a brick path to a white-walled cottage, and set his burden down. 'I live alone,' he said, unlocking the door. 'Come on in.'

He switched on the light in the tiny hall. For a moment they stared at each other. They were both bleeding from scratches on hands and faces, their clothes were covered in earth and gravel and bits of vegetation, their hair was tangled and dripping, their features were almost invisible under grime and sweat.

'A couple of survivors!' Hugh said, with a grin. 'Well, let's get cleaned up, shall we ... The bathroom's the first on the left at the top of the stairs. You can wear my dressing-gown while your things dry – it's on the back of the door. And there should be a clean towel in the airing cupboard.'

'Thanks so much,' Debbie said. She climbed the stairs, found the bathroom, and started to run a bath. The water was hot from an electric heater and there was plenty of it. She shed her clothes and lowered herself into the water with a sigh of thankfulness. She was too tired to think now about the incredible events of the day. For the moment, all that mattered was that she'd found sanctuary. She lay still, soaking away her aches and pains. Her eyes closed ...

The next thing she was aware of was a voice calling up the stairs to ask if she was still alive. She sat up, then, and scrubbed herself. She felt better for the few minutes' sleep. Afterwards she found a brush and comb and did the best she could with her hair. She looked at her sodden pile of clothes, looked again in the airing-cupboard, then went to the door in Hugh's dressing-gown. 'May I borrow one of your shirts and a pair of pants?' she called down.

Hugh appeared at the foot of the stairs, a glass in his

hand. 'Help yourself,' he said.

'Have you got any safety pins?'

'Safety pins? I doubt it – but I'll look . . .' She heard him rummaging. Presently he returned. 'You're in luck,' he said. 'A whole packet . . . Catch!'

She pinned the pants into something approaching her size, tucked in the shirt, put on some lipstick, and then went cautiously downstairs, clutching her bundle of soggy clothes and holding up the skirt of the enormous, enveloping dressing-gown like a train. Hugh regarded her quizzically.

'I know I'm a sight,' she said.

'You look quite remarkable.'

'Where can I dry my things?'

'You could put them in the oven . . . Or spread them out in front of the electric fire.'

'I think that would be better,' Debbie said.

'There's whisky in the decanter and a glass on the tray – help yourself if you feel like it. I'll be with you in a few minutes.' Hugh went off upstairs.

Debbie switched on the fire and arranged her clothes over two chair backs. She found the whisky and poured a little and gulped it down. She hated the taste of the stuff, but it had a good effect. Then she looked around.

She was in a small cluttered sitting-room. There was a sofa and an odd collection of chairs. There was an ancient roll-top desk and a lot of bookcases. The kneehole of the desk was stuffed with sheets of brown paper and files. There was a cabinet of steel drawers, and beside it a tape recorder and a record player. There was an old, scratched table, piled high with papers, letters, pipes, pens, stamps, tobacco, notebooks, a tape measure, a brimming ashtray, and a letter balance. There was also an open typewriter, with a sheet of paper in it on which there were several lines of typing. They read: 'At dusk on the night of the full moon, Bencoma concealed his warriors among the vines and mulberries at the head of the *barranco*, and waited for the unsuspecting Spaniards to approach.'

31

Debbie peeped into the kitchen. The chaos there was even worse than in the sitting-room. Dirty crockery was piled on the draining board, with a screwed-up dishcloth beside it. Unwashed saucepans were stacked on the floor. A tea towel had fallen from its hook. Debbie picked it up and put it back.

Hugh was down in a few minutes, comfortably dressed in a polo-neck sweater and a pair of corduroys. It was the first time Debbie had been able to see his face properly. He had rather blunt features, with blue eyes wrinkled at the corners. His hair was thick and unruly. He was an exceptionally big man – tall, broad, and burly. It was hard to guess his age, but she thought it might be about thirty.

He poured himself a little more whisky and dropped into a chair. 'Well, that's a bit better.'

'I can't tell you,' Debbie said, 'how grateful I am. It seems such an imposition the way I've involved you in everything. A complete stranger – and you've saved my life at least twice, and carried me miles, and looked after me ... I feel terrible – I just don't know what to say ...'

'Don't say anything,' Hugh told her. 'Just accept that it's been a quite fantastic experience. That's what I'm doing.'

'I feel I behaved so badly ...'

'My dear girl, you were terrific. Running like mad – and diving for cover without a second thought. If you'd hesitated, we'd both have been finished – I could never have fought off two blokes with iron bars ... What a couple of monsters!'

'Thank goodness you stopped in the lane, that's all.'

'If I'd known what was going to happen,' Hugh said, 'I probably wouldn't have done.'

'If *I'd* known what was going to happen, I'd never have taken that photograph.'

'M'm – you did rather ask for it, didn't you ...? Very resourceful, of course ...' Hugh reached for his pipe and began to fill it. 'How do you imagine they got on to you?'

'I can only suppose one of them came back afterwards and snooped around. They'd have had a rough idea where the flashlight went off – and I've got a plate up at the front door of the building – Still Life Studios, it says. Anyone seeing it would have been sure to connect the studio with a flash photograph being taken – and he could have got the number from the phone book.'

Hugh nodded. 'That sounds reasonable.'

'What really puzzles me,' Debbie said, 'is how they knew I'd already made a telephone call to the police.'

'If they knew you'd taken a picture of them leaving, wouldn't it have seemed pretty likely?'

'Likely, yes – but they were certain. What's more, they knew I hadn't given my name. That phoney superintendent said right away that they'd had an anonymous call. How could he possibly have known that?'

'Ah – that's a point...' Hugh pondered. 'What time did you say it was when they rang?'

'About eight o'clock.'

'Perhaps there was something in one of the papers about the police wanting to interview an anonymous caller.'

'You mean the evening papers? Do they come out so early?'

'In London, they do – the racing editions are on the streets for the early workers. If the police had told reporters about the caller immediately after you telephoned – and they'd have been anxious to get their appeal out – it could easily have been in the stop press. And one of the gang could have seen it. That's probably the explanation.'

'If so, it's a pity *I* didn't see it,' Debbie said. 'But I'd been told to stay by the telephone...' She broke off, startled. 'That's why, of course – they didn't *want* me to see a paper.'

'You saw one in the train, though. They slipped up there.'

'Yes – I suppose they had to take a chance on that. Perhaps they thought I wouldn't have time to work things out.'

'What about the radio? – the police appeal must have been on the news. Didn't you listen?'

'I began to, at one o'clock, but...' Again, Debbie stopped

abruptly. 'There was a phone call just as the news started – from a woman I didn't know. That could have been the gang – making sure I didn't hear anything.'

'It certainly fits,' Hugh agreed.

'And I couldn't have learned about the appeal any other way, because I'd been told not to talk to anyone.'

'They seem to have thought of just about everything,' Hugh said.

'Yes, don't they ... And what a nerve they had, too ...! When I think of the way that superintendent ticked me off for not giving my name – and how pleased he sounded when I told him about the photograph ... And the sergeant telling me how a man had been killed, and what had happened ... Such effrontery! It's terrifying ...'

'Well, I wouldn't let it worry you any more,' Hugh said. 'Once you've told your story to the police, it'll be up to them.'

Debbie nodded slowly. 'I suppose I will have to tell them? I know it's cowardly, but I'd much sooner not have anything more to do with it.'

'I can understand that,' Hugh said. 'After what's happened tonight, I'm sure I'd feel the same. But you'll have to tell them, if only for your own safety. Those fellows aren't going to give up because of one failure. They're obviously a formidable bunch – and you're still the key witness against them.'

'I suppose you're right ... So what do you think I ought to do? Tell the police tonight?'

'You can't do that,' Hugh said. 'There's no telephone here, and we've no transport, and you've no clothes, and we're both worn out ... It'll have to keep till tomorrow.'

'I'll certainly feel more like it tomorrow,' Debbie said.

'I think you ought to tell your parents, too.'

'I haven't any parents. They're both dead.'

'Oh ... Well, have you a brother, or a boy friend, or someone ...? You'll need a bit of support.'

Debbie shook her head. 'No one I know well – only girl friends ...'

'H'm . . . By the way, isn't it time I knew your name?'

'It's Deborah Sheldon.'

'That's a mouthful.'

'Most people call me Debbie.'

'That's better . . . I'm Hugh Freeman.'

Debbie nodded. 'You're a writer, aren't you?'

'I try to be.'

'What do you write?'

'Oh, all sorts of things. I'm working on a historical novel just now.'

'Don't you find it lonely living here by yourself?'

Hugh shrugged. 'It's not too bad . . . I go up to town and see people when I want a bit of stimulus – and I try to travel between books, when I can afford it . . . Most of the time I'm glad to be isolated. I can do as I like – nobody bothers me.'

'I'm afraid I've bothered you.'

Hugh smiled. 'I must make sure nothing of the sort occurs again!'

'Have you lived here long?'

'About a year. It's not my cottage – it belongs to my parents. I rent it from them . . . I had a room in Brighton before – I'd a romantic idea that being near the sea would help the flow of words. But it was just a distraction, and the traffic was hell . . . Look, don't you think we ought to have some food?'

'It sounds a nice idea,' Debbie said, suddenly conscious of a ferocious hunger.

'And then we can get off to bed. The spare room's a bit of a dump, but I expect you'll manage to sleep.'

'I'd sleep on a plank tonight.'

'Me, too . . . Okay, I'll scramble some eggs.'

'Do you know how?'

'Of course . . . Boil them hard and put them through the mincer.' For a moment, until he chuckled, Debbie thought he meant it.

'All the same,' she said, 'let me scramble them. It's the least I can do.'

Chapter Three

IT WAS A little after eight next morning when Hugh roused Debbie with a knock on her door and a cup of tea. 'May I come in?' he called.

'Yes,' she replied, in a sleepy voice.

He went in. She was lying deep down in the bed. All he could see of her was a tousled head and the collar of one of his shirts.

'Morning,' he said. 'I hope you slept well.'

'Wonderfully, thank you.' She studied him over the edge of the bedclothes. He was shaved and dressed and looked all set for action of some kind.

'No bad dreams?' he asked.

'No dreams at all.'

'Good ... How are the bruises?'

'I'll look when you've gone.'

He laughed. 'I thought you might like a cuppa.'

'I'd love one.'

He set it down beside her. 'There's sugar in the saucer, if you take it ... I'm off to get the car.'

'Do you think it's safe now?'

'I should think so ... I'll be careful.'

She nodded. 'Don't forget my suitcase, will you – if it's still around.'

'I won't,' he said. 'See you in about an hour.'

He picked up a heavy stick from the stand in the hall and strode off down the lane towards the quarry. The day was bright, the countryside smelt clean and fragrant after the rain, the road was empty. All around there was silence and a blessed Sunday morning peace. The intrusive violence of the night before was even harder to believe in now.

He was a little anxious about the car, but not at all about his safety. It was unlikely, he thought, that the two men would still be hanging about. Not knowing about the cottage, they'd have taken it for granted that he and

36

Debbie would seek the protection of the police right away – so it would have seemed pointless for them to stay. All the same, he approached the quarry with caution, keeping his eyes open for any sign of movement. He went first to the quarry floor and recovered Debbie's shoes – though, from the look of them, he doubted if she'd ever be able to wear them again. Then he walked slowly round the top of the wall, watching the far side. Some way before the hut he struck off through the trees, reaching the lane at the bend from which he'd first spotted Debbie. He looked out from the bushes. His own car was where he'd left it, but the other one had gone. In the distance, two boys were cycling along the lane. Otherwise, nothing stirred. The place was back to normal.

He walked quickly to the car. The rear light was shining red – it was only the headlights that he'd switched off when he'd come for the torch. He hoped the battery was all right – the engine was a devil to start by hand. He clicked off the sidelight switch and gazed around the car. Everything was in chaos. Debbie's suitcase was lying open in the back, her belongings spread over the seat. The glove compartment by the dashboard had been ransacked and its contents scattered. His driving licence, thumbed and dirty, was on the floor. It looked as though the men had been through the car with a fine comb. He tidied up, climbed in behind the wheel, and pressed the starter. The battery was low, but just as it seemed about to die, the engine fired. He drove off, much relieved.

Apart from her scratches, bruises, and blisters, Debbie felt little the worse for the ordeal she'd gone through. She was a resilient person – and this was a new day. A lovely day, too. She sat at the bedroom window in Hugh's dressing-gown, drinking her tea, listening to the birds chirruping, and thinking how attractive the garden must have looked before it became totally neglected. The outline of a lawn was still visible, late roses were blossoming on the white walls through a tangle of convolvulus, flowers were still struggling up in the weedy beds. It was really rather a shame. If the garden had been tended, the cottage would have been a dream...

She finished her tea, took a quick bath, found a pair of Hugh's slippers, and shuffled downstairs. Her sweater and skirt had dried overnight, and she brushed them clean. Then she looked around the kitchen. She couldn't possibly leave it like that. No woman could. She rolled up the sleeves of the dressing-gown, hitched the waist in tight with the cord, and got to work on the washing up. She'd just finished it when she heard the car pull up by the gate. She retreated to the bedroom and waited there until Hugh brought the suitcase up.

'Would you mind leaving it outside the door?' she called.

When she came downstairs twenty minutes later, Hugh hardly recognized her. Her hair had been swept into a smooth swathe round the back of her head, giving her an air of charming dignity; her dark blue sweater and skirt were spotless, her stockings and her smart black patent shoes impeccable. She bore no resemblance at all to the muddied, urchin girl he'd brought in the night before – nor even to the bizarre figure in the dressing-gown. She was really rather attractive, he thought. In fact, she was *very* attractive...

'Is something wrong?' she asked.

'On the contrary ...' He realized he'd been staring. 'By the way, thanks for cleaning up the kitchen.'

'I hope you didn't mind.'

'Well, I'd have done it myself, of course – sooner or later...' He grinned. 'I usually wash up between books.'

Over breakfast, Hugh suddenly said, 'You know, I think I'd better run you up to Scotland Yard myself.'

Debbie looked at him in surprise. 'That's terribly sweet of you – but it really isn't necessary. I can perfectly well get a train.'

'You don't know our Sunday service,' Hugh said. 'It can

be very tedious ... Besides, the police may want to ask me some questions, too – after all, I saw the men, and their car ...'

'You couldn't have seen much in the dark.'

'Enough to interest the police, I'm sure.'

'I'd have thought you'd have wanted to stay out of it.'

'Oh, I intend to – don't worry ... But I'd quite like to hear what they have to say first.'

Debbie still looked doubtful. 'As long as you're not doing it just for me – I owe you far too much already ... How about your work?'

'Heavens, one day won't make any difference.'

Debbie savoured the phrase. 'That sounds to me like famous last words,' she said.

They were ready to leave soon after ten. Debbie, who hadn't seen Hugh's car before in daylight, exclaimed aloud at its appearance. She wasn't normally very interested in cars, but this one, with its long, narrow body and powerful, fluted bonnet, was an eye-catcher. 'What is it?' she asked.

'A 30/98 Vauxhall – built in 1926. I'm afraid you won't find it particularly comfortable. Especially with me in it – I take up a seat and a half.'

She smiled. 'Does it go fast?'

'Not by present-day standards. It does about ninety flat out with a following wind. I share it with a bloke at the local garage – that's the only way I can afford to run it. He has it for his holidays and odd weekends – so he keeps it in running order for me. I'm not mechanically-minded, you see – I just like it because it's old and solid.'

'It looks like a monster.'

'It behaves like a monster sometimes. It's got an aeroplane engine – it's even got an altimeter! Somebody's bit of fun. The footbrake's terrible, it works on the transmission, and the engine makes a frightful din – but it's all quite amusing.'

'Well,' Debbie said, 'I'll take a chance.'

They reached London with no more than the normal incidents of the road, drove to Whitehall, and found Scotland Yard after one inquiry. Hugh, taking charge, explained to the officer on duty at the desk that they had information about the jewel robbery at Anstey's, and gave their names. The officer spoke to someone on the phone, and almost at once they were taken up to an office.

A man of about forty-five received them. He was short for a policeman, squarely-built and very tough-looking, with a military stiffness of bearing and manner. He had the steeliest grey eyes Debbie had ever seen.

'I'm Chief Superintendent Trant,' he said. 'This is Sergeant Norris...' A younger, very blond man nodded to them, and found them seats. 'Now – what's this about the jewel robbery?'

'I'm the anonymous telephone caller you wanted to see,' Debbie said.

'Is that so?' Trant looked her up and down. 'Well, I'm very glad you've decided to come forward – we'd almost given up hope ... So what can you tell me, Miss Sheldon?'

Debbie plunged into her story. This time she put in every detail she could remember, from waking in her flat on the night of the robbery to arriving exhausted at Hugh's cottage after the chase. Trant looked grim over the activities of the fake policemen, followed closely her suggestions about how the gang might have got on to her, and gave an understanding nod when she described her panic flight from the train. Very occasionally he interrupted the flow, but only to clear up a particular point. Sergeant Norris took notes, but didn't speak. Neither did Hugh, until the end, when the superintendent asked him if he could add anything, and he told about the two men arriving in the lane and what they'd said to each other. The whole recital took well over an hour.

'A remarkable story,' Trant said finally. 'And very lucidly told, if I may say so ...' He sat in silence for a few moments. 'Well now, Miss Sheldon, the first thing is to get you to look at some of our criminal records and see if you can recognize the driver of the car. The fact that the gang made this attempt on you suggests to me that he already has a police record – and that they feared you'd be able to pick him out quite easily, even without the help of the picture... Was there anything about his appearance that particularly struck you?'

'Yes,' Debbie said. 'He had an exceptionally large nose.'

'Ah – that gives us something to go on ... What about his age? Was he very young, middle-aged, or old?'

'Middle-aged, I'd say.'

'Good...' Trant glanced at the sergeant. Norris went out. Presently he returned with an armful of cards, which he put on the table in front of Debbie. 'Some of our rogues,' Trant said. 'Take your time over them – there's no hurry.'

Debbie began to look through the photographs. They were all of middle-aged men with very large noses. She flicked the cards over quite fast. She had a clear recollection of the face she was looking for, and nothing here was like it. She'd almost reached the end of the pile when, suddenly, she stopped.

'This is the man who was driving the car,' she said.

Trant took the card from her. 'Are you sure?'

'Quite sure. My photograph was almost full face – like that one.' She pointed. 'He's unmistakable. The eyes are the same, too – very close set. I've absolutely no doubt at all.'

'I see...' Trant ran his eye down the particulars on the card. 'Well, this man has quite a long criminal record. Mainly robbery, no violence. He's used various names, but the last one we heard was Clay. Harry Clay. In the underworld he's known as "Snub". He's forty-two, married, no children, keeps an ironmonger's shop in Cambridge. As far as we know, he's been behaving himself for two years...' Trant gave the card to Norris. 'If he's not in Cambridge, Sergeant, put a general call out for him.' Norris departed.

'That's a good start, anyway,' Trant said. 'Now let's see what else you can tell us, Miss Sheldon... We'll begin at the beginning. You say you saw four men at the jewellers.'

'Yes.'

'Can you describe any of the others, apart from the driver?'

'No. They were just dark shapes.'

'Height? Build? Clothes?'

'Nothing, I'm afraid.'

'What about the suitcase?'

'It looked fairly big.' Debbie extended her hands to demonstrate. 'Something like that ... I couldn't see the colour.'

'Fair enough ... Now we come to the man who telephoned you and said he was Superintendent Jenkins. What can you tell me about his voice?'

'He sounded very authoritative...' Debbie smiled. 'Rather like you ... He was very brisk and convincing. An educated voice. But there was nothing special about it. It's hard to describe a voice.'

'I agree ... Then there's the man who called for the photograph and said he was Sergeant Macey. Please describe him.'

'He was about thirty – rather tall – close-cropped fair hair – very clean-looking. A bit like Sergeant Norris. He was wearing a fawn raincoat.'

'Excellent. Now you heard his voice, of course. Could he have been the same man as the one who rang you?'

'I wouldn't think so. He spoke – well, more colloquially. He sounded quite different.'

'That seems to be two of them, then ... Now there's the woman who telephoned you when you were about to listen to the news. The call could have been pure chance, but we don't know. Anything about her?'

Debbie shook her head. 'An ordinary sort of voice. Rather high-pitched – quite well spoken.'

Trant added a note to the growing collection on his pad. 'Any resemblance to the voice of the woman who shared your compartment in the train?'

Debbie looked startled. 'None at all ... Why – do you think *she* could have been one of them?'

'Probably not, or she'd have been a bit more watchful. But one can't be sure ... Anyway, I'd like her description.'

Debbie described her. Trant made more notes.

'Finally,' he said, 'there's the man who looked into your compartment on the train. What was he like?'

Debbie thought. 'I really haven't much idea. A brown face – rather sharp-featured ... I only saw him for a second.'

'It wasn't the man who collected the photograph?'

'Oh, no.'

'Right ... So we come to you, Mr Freeman. The two men who arrived in the lane ... Anything about their voices?'

'Educated,' Hugh said. 'Urban ... No special accents.'

'Any idea what their car was?'

'A dark saloon. I can't tell you the make.'

'Could you see anything of the men?'

'Hardly a thing,' Hugh said. 'They were several yards away and mostly in darkness. I didn't see their faces at all. I couldn't even tell you whether they were old or young – except that they ran pretty fast ... The only things I saw clearly were the iron bars!'

'I can imagine ... And when they were out on the quarry floor, trying to pick up your tracks – you didn't catch a glimpse of their faces then?'

'No, they were much too far away.'

'I see ... Now you say they rummaged about in your car. Did you drive up in the car today, by any chance?'

'Yes – it's outside.'

'Do you mind if we go over it for fingerprints? We'll clean it up afterwards.'

'Oh, you needn't bother about that,' Hugh said. 'It's filthy anyway.'

'What kind is it?'

Hugh told him.

'Vintage, eh?' Trant lifted a telephone and gave some instructions. As he finished, Norris returned.

'Well now,' Trant said, 'I'm afraid we'll have to ask you to look at some more records, Miss Sheldon ... Will you take her along to the CRO, Sergeant, and see if she can pick out the man who called for the photograph ... Oh, and ask the canteen to send up sandwiches for four and a flask of coffee, will you?'

Norris nodded. Debbie got up, smiled rather wanly at Hugh, and departed with the sergeant.

'She's a good witness,' Trant said, as the door closed. 'And a brave girl. It must have been a frightful experience for her last night. She did well.'

'She certainly did,' Hugh said.

'Come to that, you didn't do badly yourself.'

'I was scared to death,' Hugh said. 'All I did was run.'

'And very wise too! There's a time to run and a time to fight ...' Trant was silent for a moment. 'About Miss Sheldon – she's going to need some sympathetic help in all this. Has she parents, do you happen to know? Relatives?'

'I gathered she hasn't anybody.'

'No boy friend? I see she doesn't wear a ring.'

'Surprisingly, no.'

'H'm ...' Again, there was a little silence. 'What's your job, Mr Freeman?'

'I write,' Hugh said.

'You mean you *just* write – nothing else?'

'Nothing else.'

'Does that fill the day for you?'

'Oh, yes ... I do an hour or two in the morning and an hour or two at night. And I walk quite a bit.'

'It sounds the life of Reilly.'

Hugh smiled. 'I wouldn't say that.'

'Is it a living?'

'Just about ... I don't have a lot of expenses.'

'From what you've told me, I take it you're not married.'

'No.'

'M'm ... Well now, Mr Freeman, you've been very forth-coming about everything, and very helpful ... Is there anything you'd like to raise with me while we're waiting for Miss Sheldon?'

'I'd be interested to know if you've made any progress

with your own inquiries,' Hugh said. 'Did the gang leave any clues?'

'Not really ... They all wore gloves, of course, and they didn't make any obvious mistakes ... We're pretty sure they were the men who did the Fawley job, but as we didn't manage to discover their identity then, that doesn't get us any further.'

'Do you think there were just the four of them in it – the men that Debbie saw?'

'I'd guess so. Four would have been ample for a comparatively simple robbery with no heavy booty to get rid of, and they wouldn't have wanted to split the proceeds more ways than they had to ... And it ties in with what we know of the Fawley raid – that also appeared to be done by four men.'

Hugh nodded. 'What about the inside help I read about?'

'Well, there was a cleaner named Willie who was employed at Anstey's until about a couple of months ago. Then he was knocked down and killed by a car that didn't stop. He could have been the one that gave them help. If so, I imagine his death wasn't an accident. Anyway, he's beyond questioning.'

'So you've actually no lead at all – apart from what Debbie's told you?'

'Not so far ... We know the man who fixed the burglar alarm must have been an electronics expert, but he's not unique in that ... Some interesting knots were used to tie up the watchman – the man who tied them might have been a sailing type ...'

'Or a lapsed Boy Scout,' Hugh said.

Trant gave a wintry smile. 'Anyway, it's a possibility we're bearing in mind. Boats are quite often used to get stolen jewellery out of the country ... Then, as you probably read, someone else did a technically perfect job blowing the strong room – but there are quite a number of gelignite experts around, so that doesn't narrow the field very much either. Far too much skilled labour is going into crime these days.'

'Don't they ever blow themselves up?'

'They do, but not often enough! The real expert has a flair for knowing just how much explosive to use. One chap I knew actually sat on the safe while he detonated the charge... Normally they blanket the operation down – at Anstey's they used the carpet from the manager's office to deaden the explosion. The only sound would have been a thump – that's why nobody heard it.'

'Where do they get the gelignite from?'

'Oh, mines and quarries. It's all stolen stuff – sometimes they knock off a hut, or maybe bribe a quarryman... There's a big underworld black market in gelignite – and I'm afraid it's getting bigger. A year or two ago a four-ounce stick cost five pounds – now it can be got for a pound. There must be hundredweights of it around.'

'Quite a headache for you,' Hugh said.

'Yes, we're always worried about jelly – especially when children get hold of it. The other day a man walked into a police station, took a couple of sticks out of his pocket and slapped them on the counter. Said he'd found a boy chalking walls with them. The kid had picked them up in a coalyard...'

'Terrifying!' Hugh said.

They talked for a little longer. Then Debbie returned with the sergeant. Norris shook his head as he entered. 'No luck, sir, I'm afraid.'

Trant didn't seem surprised. 'They'd naturally have sent someone without a record to collect the photograph, if they could – it would have cut the risk quite a bit...' He sat back. 'Well, now, Miss Sheldon, we've got to decide what to do about you ... I must say that you've been very fortunate.'

'Yes,' Debbie said. 'Thanks to Hugh.'

'I wasn't thinking only of the chase... I'm surprised the fellow who collected the photograph didn't finish you off in your studio when he had the chance.'

Debbie stared at him. 'I never thought of that...' Then she remembered. 'But he couldn't have done – not safely.'

She told Trant about the furniture removers. 'They were coming and going all day.'

'Ah – that accounts for it ... But the gang had another opportunity – last night. They could have come to the cottage.'

'They didn't know about the cottage,' Hugh said.

'I understood that they looked at your driving licence.'

Hugh frowned. 'Good lord, yes...' Then his face cleared. 'But it had my old address on it – the Brighton one. It was a three-year licence.'

'I see. The gods have certainly been watching over you... Well, we must try to make sure your good fortune lasts.' Trant looked at Debbie. 'I hardly need to tell you, Miss Sheldon, that you're still in very great danger. These men may have lost track of you for the moment – but they'll make the most strenuous efforts to find you. They've shown that very clearly... Are you prepared to place yourself under our protection?'

'I suppose I'd better,' Debbie said. 'What will you do? – put someone outside the studio?'

'Oh, I don't think you'd better go back there... For tonight, at any rate, I suggest we install you in a London hotel – under a different name, of course. We'll take you there, and one of our men will stay near you all the time and make sure you come to no harm. There'll be no expense for you – we'll look after the bill. Is that all right?'

'It's all right for tonight,' Debbie said, 'but what about tomorrow? What about my work?'

'Let's take things a step at a time, Miss Sheldon, shall we?'

Debbie looked at him blankly.

Trant turned to Hugh. 'I wonder if you'd care to stay over too, Mr Freeman? You'd be a bit of company for Miss Sheldon – and I dare say I shall want to talk to you again in the morning. What do you say?'

'It's up to Debbie,' Hugh said. 'I'm quite willing.'

'I'd be glad,' Debbie said.

'Then I'll certainly stay... What about my car, Superintendent?'

'That'll be all right till tomorrow, Mr Freeman ... We won't tow it away!'

The arrangements were soon made. At Trant's suggestion, Hugh booked the hotel rooms himself, giving the names of Miss Johnson and Mr Forbes. Someone fetched Debbie's suitcase from the Vauxhall. Sergeant Norris found a case for Hugh and managed to rustle up a toothbrush, razor, and pyjamas from some secret store. Trant introduced the man who would discreetly keep an eye on them – another sergeant named Everett. He was a big, blue-suited, bald-headed man who looked like a prosperous company director. Afterwards Hugh and Debbie both had their fingerprints taken, as a check against any that might be found on the Vauxhall. The superintendent issued his one categorical instruction for the night – that Debbie shouldn't go outside the hotel or communicate with anyone. Then Norris took them down a back staircase to his own car and drove them to the hotel. It was just before seven when they arrived. They registered in their new names, and were shown to neighbouring rooms.

Hugh paused at Debbie's door. 'As all this is going to come out of the public purse,' he said, 'I suggest we meet downstairs in ten minutes and have a drink.'

'That's a good idea,' Debbie said. 'I need one.'

Chapter Four

THERE WERE only a few customers in the spacious bar when Hugh looked in. He picked a quiet corner, lit his pipe, and sat down to wait for Debbie. He knew just when she was about to arrive because Sergeant Everett sauntered in first. The sergeant took a seat on the far side of the room, called for a lager, and opened the *Sunday Telegraph*. A moment later, Debbie appeared. She'd put on the smart dress she'd packed for the Eastbourne hotel – it was of charcoal grey wild silk, very simply cut – and she was wearing a pair of exotic antique earrings. Hugh thought she looked terrific – or would have done if her expression had been less unhappy.

'What would you like to drink?' he asked, as she joined him.

'Martini, please.'

He beckoned the waiter and ordered two large ones. When they came, he raised his glass to her. 'At least this is better than being chased through a quarry,' he said.

Only a flicker of response showed in her face. She downed half the drink and groped rather desperately in her bag for a cigarette.

Hugh lit it for her. 'Cheer up, Debbie ... This isn't going to last for ever.'

'That's just the trouble,' she said. 'I think it may.'

'What do you mean?'

'Well, it's obvious, isn't it? As long as I'm around, that man Clay isn't safe – so I'm not safe either. And things could go on like that indefinitely.'

'Oh, I shouldn't think so,' Hugh said. 'With a face as distinctive as his, he'll probably be picked up pretty soon, wherever he is. Then he'll be tried and convicted and the gang will have no further interest in you.'

'Doesn't it take a long while to get a man convicted?'

'Well – yes ... Quite a while.'

'How long?'

'I don't know exactly – I think it depends on how much evidence has to be collected. First he has to be committed for trial ... A few weeks, I suppose, till he's safely put away.'

'There you are – a few *weeks* ...! Even after he's caught. And all that time I'll have to be lying low somewhere.'

'It does look rather like it,' Hugh said.

'But, Hugh, I just can't do that. I've got stacks of work waiting – things I've promised to clients. They're relying on

49

me. I can't just walk out on my commitments – my name will be mud.'

'You can tell them what happened, when it's all over. They'll understand.'

'I dare say – but by then they'll have taken their work somewhere else, won't they? They'll have made new arrangements... The business will have gone to pot, and I'll have to start all over again from the beginning.'

Hugh nodded slowly. 'It could be rough, I agree. I do sympathize, Debbie – believe me, I do. All the same...'

'All the same, what?'

'Well, there's no doubt about the danger – and it's better to lose your business than your life.'

'I know that – but it's not much consolation. All that work...! Honestly, I *slaved* for the first six months. You can't imagine how I feel.'

'I can, you know,' Hugh said. 'I once spent six months on a story and then lost the only manuscript.'

'Did you really...? That must have been terrible. Like Carlyle and *The French Revolution*.'

'The loss was the only resemblance, I assure you.'

'What did you do?'

'Gloomed for a week – then started to write it again. What else could I do...? Actually, it turned out better the second time.'

Debbie sighed. 'I suppose I'll manage, too – somehow. Anyway, it's no good going on about it... Do you think the public purse will run to another drink?'

'If it won't, the private one will.' Hugh called the waiter and ordered more Martinis. 'How did you come to start your business, Debbie?'

'I won a photographic competition – that was the beginning of it. All of a sudden I had a bit of a name in the technical journals and seven hundred and fifty pounds in the bank... I'd always thought I'd like to work on my own one day – doing the things I wanted, in the way I wanted – and this seemed the moment to try my luck. I used the money to rent a studio and buy some equipment, wrote

round to people I knew, got myself an agent, and began ...
And I've been slogging away like mad ever since.'

'I suppose that's why you've had no time for boy friends,'
Hugh said.

Debbie smiled. 'It wasn't just a question of time – I wasn't
interested...' She made a large hole in her second drink.
'Do you want to hear about my love life?'

'It's always a fascinating subject.'

'Well, when I was eighteen I fell in love with a married
man. It was a very pure, romantic attachment, because he
was much older than I was and he wouldn't take advantage
of an innocent girl. But naturally, it didn't get me anywhere
at all. It was very frustrating... After three years of that, I
happened to meet and fall for someone of my own age. He
was a sculptor, and a very talented one – only he didn't
sculpt much. He had a brother who was a stage designer,
and both of them had a great many friends who were all
talented in one way or another. But none of them did any
work. They used to spend all their time lying around listening to music – in my flat, while I was out at my bourgeois
job. Gradually it dawned on me that I was financing them.
It was fun staying up half the night listening to Beethoven
and Bach, I'll admit – but, came the dawn, I was the one
who had to rush off and earn the rent. Even when Max –
the sculptor – did earn any money, it didn't seem to occur
to him to spend any of it on me. Or us. It was clothes for
himself, and drinks for the crowd. He liked a communal
life, you see.' Debbie's eyes crinkled at the corners. ' "He
bowed and smiled a friendly grin, and brought his hungry
family in." Poor Max! How mean I sound, don't I? Anyway, I walked out on them all one day. And then, not long
after, I got the money for the competition – by which time I
was in the mood for some constructive work and an orderly
life, I guess.'

'And no men. I can imagine...' Hugh sipped his drink.
'Just as well you didn't marry him, wasn't it?'

'Oh, I would have done. Like a shot. But in those circles
the word marriage was never mentioned. I began to feel it

was a flaw in myself that I even thought of it...!' Debbie brushed a speck of ash from her dress. 'Now let's talk about you for a change. Why haven't *you* married?'

'I'd make a lousy husband,' Hugh said.

'Why?'

'No woman would put up with me for a day. I'm a manic depressive.'

'Are you really? How alluring that sounds!'

'It's true... When I'm not writing, I'm fine. I sing in my bath, telephone my friends, go and see people, enjoy conversation, laugh like a drain – oh, I'm a hell of a good fellow... But when I'm writing – then I'm really shocking. I'm bad-tempered, irritable, morose. I avoid my friends. I don't speak to anyone. I smoke myself sick. I can't sleep. I think I'm going to die. At night I leap up and down like a kangaroo, scribbling madly... In fact, I'm just a pain in the neck... Anyway, I could never stand a woman building a nest round me.'

Debbie laughed. 'You know,' she said, 'I think I'm beginning to feel better.'

'Good!'

'You're a bit given to exaggeration, aren't you?'

'Sometimes... It goes with the trade. But what I've just said is true enough.'

'I'd like to hear about the trade,' Debbie said. 'When did you start writing?'

'Oh, years ago, when I was a kid. I always had the urge. I was sending short stories to magazines when I was fourteen... I must have been a loathsome child.'

'How many books have you written?'

'Two a year for eight years.'

'In your own name?'

'No, I use various pseudonyms. I write the historical novels as Mark Avery.'

'Mark Avery... That seems to ring a bell...'

Hugh smiled. 'You don't have to pretend. If there's any bell, it's probably tolling...! Hardly anyone knows about me.'

'Well, I'm sure they will,' Debbie said.

'How can you be sure? You don't know how I write.'

'I can guess from the way you talk. And you've got years ahead of you – and lots of energy . . . What do the reviewers say about you?'

'Not much. When they do break silence, they're usually critical.'

'Does that worry you?'

'Less than it used to. And sometimes they're quite help-ful. Anyway, a writer has to learn to take it. If he can't stand the heat, he shouldn't go into the kitchen.'

'Why do you use pseudonyms?'

'Partly because I write different kinds of books. The reader likes to know what to expect – and the pseudonym's a sort of brand name . . . Partly because a story reveals so much about the author – it's like undressing in public. Pseudonimity makes one's defects less shaming.'

'Some authors don't seem to mind.'

'Perhaps they've less to be ashamed of,' Hugh said. 'Or else they're more exhibitionist.'

'M'm . . . What's this novel you're writing at the moment – or is that a secret?'

'It's a load of nonsense, actually. It just won't seem to go right.'

'How far have you got?'

'Four chapters – and I hate them all.'

'Why – what's the trouble?'

'Me, I guess . . . The characters won't come to life, the dialogue seems unreal . . . I think I'm a bit stale – perhaps I need a change of scene.'

'What's the book about?'

'It's supposed to be about the conquest of the Guanches by the Spaniards – the Guanches were the original in-habitants of Tenerife . . . But I'm having to make most of it up – there isn't much reliable source material.'

'It sounds an interesting subject,' Debbie said.

'Oh, there's nothing wrong with the subject – if only I could get it down. The background's good, too. Tenerife's a

53

very dramatic island – and very colourful.'

'What about romance?'

'That's all laid on. There was a Guanche princess named Dacil who fell in love with one of the conquistadores. She was a beautiful girl. She had corn-coloured hair and very dark eyes – "dark eyes that go to the heart", someone wrote – and a complexion like rose petals.'

'You sound quite attached to her . . . I believe you prefer your heroines to real people.'

Hugh grinned. 'Well, you do tend to get a more satisfying type of woman,' he said.

Chapter Five

AT ABOUT THE time that Hugh and Debbie were taking their first drink, Superintendent Trant was preparing to leave his office. His desk and his professional conscience were both clear. He'd done a huge day's work on the Anstey case. He'd made far more progress than he'd expected. He'd assured the safety of his chief witness. There was nothing more to be gained by hanging on at the Yard. For once he could get home at a reasonable hour – to his wife, a civilized meal and an early night.

Trant was a dedicated man – dedicated to the suppression of crime. Not petty crime – others could take care of that – but major crime, the kind that could bring down the pillars of society if it went unchecked. Particularly violent crime . . .

He was ambitious, as well as dedicated. And with good reason. He was a Chief Superintendent at a phenomenally early age. He knew his talents and capacities, and he aimed at the highest post in the service. But ambition wasn't his main driving force. He had a deep, philosophical hatred of men who made ruthless war on society for their own ends. He was the opposite of an anarchist. He believed in order.

Only against a background of order could the human race hope to lead fruitful and satisfying lives.

Like Hugh Freeman, he had good hopes that a man as conspicuous as Harry Clay would soon be picked up. And he desperately wanted him to be picked up. The thing that worried him most about this jewel gang was the cumulative killing. Three murders and an attempted murder in less than six months – that was his reckoning. Two of them unnecessary murders – committed with indifference, as other men would swat a fly. The casual liquidation of something only slightly in the way. And the indifference could spread. In fact, it was spreading. In all his working career, Trant had never known so much pointless violence in the underworld. If he could catch Clay, and pin a life sentence on him, that might make some of the others think twice....

Not that he expected to hear anything about Clay for a while. In a day or two, with luck, some hopeful lead might come in – some report from an observant citizen, some tip-off from the informer network, something from Interpol. But not yet... He was all the more surprised when, just as he was putting on his hat to leave, Sergeant Norris came rushing in with news.

'Message from the Epping police, sir,' the sergeant said. 'They say a man named Harry Clay is in Epping Cottage Hospital after a road crash. Seems he answers to the description we circulated in connection with the Anstey job.'

Trant instantly forgot his supper, his wife, and his bed. 'Let's go,' he said.

Arrangements had been made by the Yard while they were on their way. They were met at the hospital by the secretary, George Meakin, and the Essex police sergeant who'd investigated the car crash – an officer named Grange. Trant said, 'Before we talk, I'd better check that he really is our man, if that's all right with you, Mr Meakin.' The secretary nodded. Trant followed him to the ward door and Meakin indicated the third bed on the left. Trant went in alone and walked slowly up the ward. The man in the bed was dozing. Trant stopped for a moment and scrutinized him. He saw at once that this was the Harry Clay of the record card. As the girl had said, the huge nose, the narrow-set eyes, were unmistakable. An ugly-looking customer, in every way...

He rejoined the others. 'Yes, that's the fellow... When did the crash happen, Sergeant?'

'We don't know exactly, sir,' Grange said. 'There was no other car involved, so no one reported it at the time. He was brought in here around five-thirty yesterday morning.'

'Five-thirty, eh? That fits... Right – tell me about the crash.'

'It was on a minor road, sir, going through Epping Forest.' Grange spread out a map he'd brought with him and indicated the place. 'Clay was travelling in a northerly direction in a Hillman Minx – his own car, according to the log book. Apparently it skidded off the road at a bend. It ploughed between some trees and overturned in a hollow. After that it wasn't visible from the road. The first anyone knew about the accident was when the driver of another car saw an injured man sitting by the roadside, just before five-thirty. He drove the man here, and the hospital informed us about the crash.'

Trant looked at the secretary. 'How badly is he hurt?'

'Multiple bruises and a nasty crack on the head,' Meakin said. 'Nothing serious – but he was very confused and suffering from shock when he came in.'

'How is he now?'

'He's coming along – he'll be able to get up in a day or two... By the way, he was in an extraordinarily filthy condition when he arrived – looked as though he'd been burrowing in mud. Hands, clothes, shoes – everything. I asked him how he'd got like that but he said he couldn't remember.'

'That's interesting...' Trant was silent for a moment. 'Did you get in touch with anyone? His wife?'

'Yes – the Cambridge police contacted her at home yesterday morning and she arrived here in the afternoon.'

'Did she talk to Clay?'

'Not yesterday – he was under sedation and sleeping. She was here again this evening and had a chat with him – you only just missed her. She's staying at the Blue Boar in Epping if you want to get hold of her.'

Trant nodded. 'Right – let's go and talk to him ourselves ... I think we'd better have a screen.' There was a short pause while a nurse set up screens round the bed and arranged four chairs. By that time, the patient was fully awake.

Trant seated himself near the head of the bed. 'We're police officers,' he said.

Clay eyed him from under his bandage. 'What d'you want?'

'We want to know about your crash.'

'What – again?'

'Yes.'

'I couldn't help what happened. The road was slippery.'

'Where had you come from, and where were you going?'

'I'd come from Cambridge – that's where I live. I was going to Portsmouth.'

'Why?'

'I was going to look at a shop.... What's all this about, anyway? You've got nothing on me.'

'We used to have,' Trant said.

'So what? I've been going straight for years.'

'That remains to be seen. Why were you going to look at a shop?'

'I was thinking of buying it, if you must know. The wife doesn't like it in Cambridge any more – says it's too cold for her. Wants to move south, see? Well, she saw an ad. – ironmonger's shop up for sale in Portsmouth. That's our line – ironmongery. So I was going to give the place the once over ... That satisfy you?'

'What was the name of the shop?'

'Clarkson's. Harbour Street.'

'Were they expecting you?'

'No – I was going to drop in.'

'Some drop!' Trant said.

'Why not...? Bit of an outing.'

'What time did you leave Cambridge?'

'About half past three, Saturday morning.'

'Rather an early start, wasn't it?'

'I was aiming to miss the traffic – you know what it's like, Saturdays.'

'Did anyone see you leave? Or hear you?'

'Yes, the wife.'

'Anyone else?'

'How would I know...? I don't reckon so.'

'Too bad,' Trant said. 'Did you stop on the way anywhere? Talk to anyone? Buy any petrol?'

'Not at that time in the morning. I just kept going.'

'What were you doing on that by-road in the Forest? That was an odd way to go to Portsmouth, wasn't it?'

'I thought I'd take a short cut. Across to Waltham Abbey from A11... But I got lost.'

'Was that why you were driving too fast?'

'I told you, the road was slippery.'

'What exactly happened?'

'I don't remember,' Clay said. 'All I know is, there was a bend, and I felt the car going off the road ... Next thing I knew, I was sitting by the roadside and a bloke in a car was calling out to me.'

'You don't remember anything in between?'

'Not a sausage.'

'I'm told you were covered with mud when you were found – plastered from head to foot. How did you get like that?'

'How d'you think? It was a muddy place where I crashed.'

'Were you thrown out of the car into the mud?'

Clay hesitated. 'No – I reckon I must have climbed out somehow – but I don't remember. Maybe I wandered around a bit and got muddy that way.'

'I see... Well, Clay, it probably won't surprise you to hear that I'm taking you into custody.'

Clay looked very surprised indeed – and very indignant 'What for? What's the charge?'

'For the moment, being concerned in a jewel robbery at Anstey's on Friday night. And I have to warn you . . .'

'Aw, skip that stuff. You're nuts. I don't know a thing about any jewel robbery. It's like I told you – I was going to Portsmouth.'

'Well, now you're going to a prison hospital,' Trant said. 'Will you stay with him, Sergeant Grange? – I'll make the arrangements.'

The three men filed out. 'I'd like to use your phone, Mr Meakin, if I may,' Trant said. The secretary showed him to the office and left him there.

He was back in a few minutes. 'That's all fixed,' he said. 'There'll be a police ambulance here in half an hour . . . Now I wonder if I could see the shoes Clay was wearing when he came in?'

An orderly fetched them. Trant and Norris examined them together. The leather was almost invisible under a coating of dried mud. The soles were smooth, the heels rubber-tipped.

'Right,' Trant said. 'We'll be collecting all Clay's things when we take him away, Mr Meakin – perhaps you could have them ready. That's all for the moment – and I'm much obliged to you for your help . . .' He turned to Norris. 'Okay, let's take a look at the scene of the crash.'

In the car, he said, 'Any idea what I'm thinking, Sergeant?'

'I guess so, sir.'

'Let's hope we're right,' Trant said.

With the help of Grange's map, they had no difficulty in finding the place where the Hillman had crashed. It was a lonely spot, deep in the heart of the forest, featureless except for the trees. The car was lying on its roof a few yards from the verge. As Grange had said, it was invisible from the road because of the hollow. The bodywork was battered, the windscreen broken. The door by the driver's seat was hanging open. One of the rear doors was open, too. There was no obvious reason why it should have been, since the lock was intact. Tyre marks on the road showed where the skid had started. The surface, under its canopy of trees, was damp. Trant guessed it was almost always damp there.

He flashed a torch inside the car and into the boot, but found nothing of interest. He studied the ground around the car. It was wet and soft – but hardly muddy enough to account for Clay's state. There were a lot of footmarks. Some of them were easily identifiable as Clay's. Trant cast around, trying to see where the man had walked. He lost the footmarks in a patch of grass, then found them again. They seemed to lead into the forest . . .

Chapter Six

DEBBIE LAY in bed in her hotel room, reviewing the day's events as she usually did before she went to sleep.

She felt much better about everything than she had done a few hours before. No doubt the bottle of wine she'd shared with Hugh over a leisurely dinner had helped. But it wasn't in her nature, in any case, to dwell for long on situations that she couldn't change. Already she'd begun to look ahead in a practical way, wondering if and when Superintendent Trant would let her write to her clients, and what she could say to them without giving anything away.

It was a relief not to feel afraid any more. She could sleep soundly, knowing that she was now in the safe hands of the genuine police. Trant was a man who inspired complete confidence. And Hugh and Sergeant Everett were occupying the rooms on either side of her.

So she must get to sleep. The best way to compose her mind, she knew from experience, was to concentrate on some warm and comforting thought. Tonight, she thought of Hugh. She'd enjoyed her evening with him, in spite of her troubles. In fact, she'd enjoyed the whole day. They'd got on extraordinarily well together. In a way they were birds of a feather. She wasn't as creative as he was – but they were both individualists, both out on their own ... It was quite ridiculous – but meeting him had made the horrible happenings of the past twenty-four hours seem almost worth while. She smiled to herself, remembering some of the things he'd said. Pretending that no woman could stand him, when what he really wanted was to be free to do as he liked ... A difficult man, of course, but interesting. And interesting-looking. As she lay there in the darkness she could recall his features with photographic clarity. The broad, good-humoured face, the quizzical eyes, the firm jaw line that suggested strength – or obstinacy – behind the gentleness. An attractive man ... She'd enjoyed dancing with him after dinner ... It was strange how big men could be so light on their feet when they danced ...

Very soon, she slept.

In the morning she decided to skip breakfast and have a quick hair-do in the hotel salon. She emerged to find Hugh waiting for her in the lobby with a copy of the *Daily Mail* in his hand and a look of extreme satisfaction on his face. 'What do you think of this?' he said.

She took the paper and read the headline. JEWEL ROBBERY MAN CHARGED, it said. Below, there was a short paragraph mentioning Harry Clay by name and referring to the car accident that had led to his arrest in Epping Hospital.

'What a stroke of luck!' she exclaimed.

'Isn't it ...? At least, Debbie, you can see the end of the tunnel now – even if it is going to take you a few weeks to get there.'

'It's marvellous! I certainly didn't think anything would happen quite so soon ... I wonder where he was going?'

'Home to Cambridge, I should think. Epping would have been on the route ...'

They were still discussing the news when a page boy called for 'Mr Forbes'. It was Trant on the telephone, to say he'd like to see them both and that Sergeant Norris was on his way to collect them. The sergeant arrived ten minutes later in his little car and whisked them to the Yard.

Trant greeted them with one of his on-and-off smiles, said he hoped they'd had a restful night, and got briskly down to business.

'I've a lot of things to discuss with you,' he said. 'You'll have heard about Clay, of course?'

Debbie nodded. 'It's splendid, isn't it?'

'Yes, we were extremely fortunate. I expect you'd like to hear what happened...' Trant told them about the call from the Essex police, and his inquiries afterwards. 'Clay naturally isn't admitting anything,' he said, 'and neither is his wife, but all the facts confirm your identification of him, Miss Sheldon, as the man you photographed. The place and time of the accident tie in well with his having driven the sixteen miles from London after the robbery. He hasn't any solid evidence to back up his account of his movements. He was obviously avoiding main roads to keep out of the way of the police, not to escape the traffic – and he crashed because he was over-anxious about his getaway. It all fits. He's undoubtedly our man.'

'What's the significance of the mud on him?' Hugh asked.

'Oh, I think I've got the explanation of that...' The superintendent sounded a trifle smug this morning. 'I don't believe for a moment that Clay got himself into that state as a result of the accident, or just by walking around. The hospital secretary used the phrase "burrowing in mud" – and I think that's just what he had been doing. My guess is that he had the suitcase of jewels in his car. Because of the crash, he had to hide them... I believe he got muddy because he buried them in the Forest.'

'Really...?' Hugh frowned. 'You think he could have done – in spite of his injuries?'

'The doctor says he could. He was probably dazed, but he was still capable of making a considerable physical effort.

62

That's the medical view, anyway.'

'Wouldn't he have left tracks?'

'Well, up to a point, he did,' Trant said. 'He certainly walked in the Forest – there's a lot of soft ground, and in places his footmarks are quite plain. Sergeant Norris and I managed to follow them for some distance. But there's a lot of high ground, too, that shows nothing – and that's where we lost them. An additional complication is that yesterday was a fine Sunday and there were a great many visitors out. They trampled over everything like a herd of buffaloes – particularly in the neighbourhood of the wrecked car. We've tried tracker dogs, but the trail seems to be cold. So far as recovering the stuff is concerned, we're up against it . . . The Forest's a vast place.'

'But Clay couldn't have gone far into it, could he . . .? He wouldn't have had time.'

'You'd be surprised,' Trant said. 'I've been working it out . . . If he left Anstey's at four, he'd have reached the Forest by half past four at the latest, even allowing for the switch of cars. And he wasn't found till half past five. That means he could have walked for half an hour before hiding the stuff. It's true he had the suitcase to carry, but he's a tough, strong man – I'd still give him a possible radius of a mile. That's a lot of ground when you don't know the direction. No doubt we'll cover it in time – but it's going to be rather like looking for a needle in a haystack.'

'Yes, I see . . .' Hugh pondered. 'I suppose you are right about the case . . .? I must say I wouldn't have expected the gang to allow one man to take the jewels away on his own.'

'They probably had no choice,' Trant said. 'Whatever plans they'd made would have had to be hastily recast when they realized they'd been photographed. We know that at least two of them, and possibly three, were occupied with Miss Sheldon all day. I imagine they didn't have an extra man to spare. Anyway, these crooks don't usually double-cross each other. They know it isn't safe.'

'I'll bet it's not,' Hugh said.

There was a little pause.

'Of course,' Trant went on, 'the fact that Clay *was* alone with the jewels – assuming he was – raises a rather interesting question about what happens next. Obviously the gang will want to recover the suitcase. No doubt Clay has a pretty good idea himself where he buried it – but the gang hasn't. And Clay is in custody, so he can't tell them . . .'

Hugh broke in. 'You said he talked to his wife, Superintendent – and she's probably in on the job. Wouldn't he have told her? And she'd have told the gang.'

'He'd have tried to, I'm sure . . . The thing is, could he have described the place in such a way that the gang would find it? It's one thing to go back yourself over ground you've covered, and quite another to pinpoint a spot in words – particularly if it lies deep in a forest, and you were rather dazed at the time, and it wasn't properly light – which it wouldn't have been at that hour. I'd say the chances are a hundred to one that Clay wasn't able to give adequate verbal instructions . . . If that's so, it means that the gang won't be able to lay their hands on the jewels until Clay is free again. And as the final charge against him will include murder as well as robbery, that won't be for at least twenty years . . . Unless, of course, he's acquitted . . .'

'But he won't be acquitted, surely,' Debbie said.

'Not if you're around to give your evidence, Miss Sheldon – he hasn't got a chance . . . Without your evidence, I think he *would* be acquitted – in fact, I doubt if he'd even be sent for trial. Any good lawyer would get him off. *We* know his story isn't true – but he has got a story. He even had a trade paper in his pocket with an advertisement of the Portsmouth shop ringed in blue pencil – there's planning for you! He's got a kind of explanation for everything that happened, and we can't prove he was lying – without you. The whole case will turn on your identification of him – your first-hand identification, made during a personal appearance by you in court, where your evidence can be tested and weighed in cross-examination. No jury could be relied on to convict on anything less, on anything second-hand, in view of the lack of other evidence ... The position is, therefore, that you – and you alone – stand between the gang and half a million pounds' worth of booty. You were in danger before, when you were merely threatening the freedom of one of the gang. You're in much greater danger now, because the stake for all of them has enormously increased. If they're ever to get the jewels, they've simply *got* to prevent you giving evidence.'

Debbie took the new situation calmly. 'The amount of danger doesn't really make much difference, does it?' she said. 'I mean, I'd have had to be closely guarded anyway, wouldn't I, until Clay was convicted – I more or less reconciled myself to that last night. The thing is, where are you going to keep me?'

'That's something I'm thinking hard about,' Trant said. 'The hotel's safe enough for a day or two – but for a longer stay I'd prefer to get you out of London. There's an empty lodge on an estate in Hertfordshire that might do – I'm looking into that. Whatever we decide on, it should be some spot not too far from town, because we may want to talk to you from time to time. Preferably some isolated place, where the guard will be able to to keep a good look-out all round.'

'It *is* going to be jolly,' Debbie said.

'It would be much better, of course, if you could take someone along with you ... Have you, by any chance, a friend who'd be prepared to shut herself up for a few weeks?'

Debbie shook her head. 'Not a hope, I'm afraid ... They're all working girls.'

'Well, we'll have to try and fix you up with a companion. Perhaps the wife of one of the local policemen. Or someone from the Yard ...'

Debbie made one final effort. 'I suppose there's no chance I could go on with some of my work there?'

'It would depend on the kind of work, Miss Sheldon. You could certainly do a bit of indoor photography – I expect we could rig up a dark-room for you and get you everything you needed... But obviously if your clients were in touch with you, and knew where you were, the whole point of taking you to a secret place would be lost.'

'Couldn't I write to them as though I were still at the studio – and have someone collect their answers and bring them to me?'

'Oh, I'd be very much against that. We can't afford to have any trail leading to you.'

'I suppose not...' Debbie sighed. 'Anyway, it would be pretty hopeless – I do so much of my arranging on the telephone... All right, Superintendent, I suppose there's no help for it – I'll just have to let the business go down the drain.'

'I'm extremely sorry,' Trant said. 'I'm afraid it can't be avoided... However, it may be some consolation to you to know that you won't be involved in any financial sacrifice. If you're prepared to co-operate with us, and give your evidence at the trial, I can assure you that you'll be very generously compensated for any loss – to the point of making certain that you'll be able to start up your business again with good prospects.'

'Well, that softens the blow,' Debbie said.

Hugh looked surprised. 'Are you really in a position to guarantee that, Superintendent? Off your own bat – just like that? It could cost you a packet.'

'It isn't only my guarantee,' Trant said. 'And nothing that I'm doing is "off my own bat" – the decisions are being taken at a very high level indeed. I've been appointed – how shall I put it? – a kind of Supremo, in this very tough and vital case... You know the position about crime in this country at the moment. It's paying big dividends. The gangs are well-organized, well-off, and highly intelligent. They're recruiting better brains and better skills every day. They're having more successes in their battle with society. Sometimes it looks as though they'll come out on top... Well, we've got to turn the tide. We've got to show them that they can't get away with it. We've got to demonstrate that the police are smarter than they are, that they're going to be caught. What we need is a resounding victory – and in this particular case I think it's possible ... Which brings me to the point I've been working up to all morning. I'm hoping for the assistance of both of you in a plan I have.'

'And what is that?' Debbie asked.

'This gang must be quite desperate now to get rid of you, Miss Sheldon. Because of that, I think I may be able to tempt them into a trap.'

Hugh looked at Trant a bit warily. 'What's in your mind, Superintendent?'

'Briefly,' Trant said, 'I propose to arrange a stand-in for Miss Sheldon. A young woman who at a distance could be mistaken for her. She will be the bait. She will be hidden away under guard in a different place from Miss Sheldon – but in her case, steps will be taken to let the gang discover where the place is. At some point, I have no doubt, they'll appear on the scene. The stand-in will show herself, with proper safeguards, and be identified as Miss Sheldon – which, incidentally, will take the heat off the real Miss Sheldon. The gang will then move into action – and so shall we. With luck, we shall get them all.'

There was a slightly startled silence. Then Hugh said, 'That's a mighty big superstructure to build on a slim theory, isn't it?'

'A slim theory ...?'

'Why, yes ... After all, you're only guessing that Clay had the jewels with him, and that he buried them, and that he wasn't able to indicate where he'd hidden them ... It's an interesting idea – but you don't *know*.'

'On the evidence,' Trant said, 'it's a very reasonable guess. I forgot to mention that we found the back door of the car hanging open – which suggests that something was taken out. Then there was the mud on Clay, and the tracks ... And I've told you why I think he couldn't have pinpointed the place.'

'The car door could have been opened by anybody,' Hugh said. 'One of those Sunday visitors you were talking about ... And, if Clay was dazed, he *might* have fallen into a ditch and covered himself with mud struggling out ... Or, if he did bury the stuff, he might have made a mental note of some feature – some specially shaped tree – and been able to describe the place exactly ... I'm not saying any of these things happened – all I'm saying is that your plan doesn't seem to me to have very solid foundations. For all you know, the suitcase may have been entrusted to some other member of the gang. Or they may already have found it in the Forest and dug it up ... Your plan could be a complete waste of effort.'

'I don't think it will be,' Trant said. 'In any case, I'm prepared to take the chance. It may be a bit of a gamble – but it's a gamble where we've nothing to lose and everything to gain. If I'm wrong and nothing happens we'll be no worse off ... And I've a very strong hunch that I'm right. I think the gang will show up – and I think they'll go for the bait.'

'What do you expect them to do – launch an armed attack on the place?'

'I would think that very likely – since it'll seem the only way open to them of achieving their objective ... I certainly hope so. Unless and until they attack, we shan't know that they are the gang, and we shan't be able to deal with them.'

'H'm ... I must say the imagination boggles. I know they're pretty desperate characters and I know they planned to kill Debbie in the country. But going for an unprotected girl is one thing – attacking her when she's under police guard is quite another.'

'If the train robbers were prepared to attack Durham Jail,' Trant said, 'why shouldn't jewel robbers be prepared to attack a house? – a much less formidable proposition. In the context of today's violent crime, there's nothing extraordinary about it.'

Hugh shrugged. 'Well, it's your affair. Personally, I couldn't be more sceptical.'

There was a pause as the argument reached deadlock.

Then Debbie said, 'Who's going to be the stand-in, Superintendent? Have you got someone in mind?'

'Yes,' Trant said. 'One of our young policewomen. She's a brunette like you, Miss Sheldon, and about your build... The problem will be to make her appear convincing – to someone, say, watching her through binoculars from three hundred yards away. That won't be easy – and that's where I'll need your help. There'll have to be quite a bit of rehearsing. Your hairstyle will have to be copied, and the girl will need to study your way of walking around, and your gestures. And she'll have to borrow some of your clothes – those that the gang have already seen you wearing... It'll all be a bit of a nuisance for you, I'm afraid.'

'I don't mind,' Debbie said. 'At least it will help to pass the time.'

'Good – that's settled, then...' Trant turned to Hugh again. 'Now we come to you, Mr Freeman.'

'What about me?'

'I'd appreciate it if you'd join the group at this second establishment I've mentioned.'

'What on earth for?' Hugh said. 'I'd be no use to you... In fact, if things did turn out the way you expect, I'd be a positive hindrance. I'm a peace-loving chap – I'd be worse than useless in a fight.'

Trant regarded him thoughtfully. 'You don't look as though you'd be useless.'

'I'm telling you... I always run away from violence.'

'H'm... Well, as it happens, you'd be strictly a noncombatant. I don't want you for anything violent.'

'Then why *do* you want me?'

'For several reasons... I won't go into them all now – they'll emerge later. But you can take it from me that they're good ones. A very important one is that you'll enormously strengthen the deception we're trying to put over. The gang will remember your very distinctive car, they'll see you around, they'll think it quite natural you should have stayed to help an attractive girl like Miss

69

Sheldon – and the fact that you *are* around will convince them that she's there.'

'If they come,' Hugh said.

'They'll come.'

Hugh shook his head. 'I'm sorry, but I just can't take this project seriously... And I certainly don't fancy tying myself up for weeks without a jolly good reason.'

'Could there be a better reason than the possible destruction of a dangerous gang?'

'It's not my line of country,' Hugh said. 'I'm a natural bystander.'

'You weren't a bystander when you helped Miss Sheldon in the quarry.'

'That was different. It was a personal situation. And there was no one else...'

'Don't you want to see this gang destroyed?'

'Of course I do – but in my view gangs should be destroyed by the people whose job it is... If you think this plan of yours will help to do it, that's up to you – but I'd sooner you counted me out.'

'As a citizen, Mr Freeman, you have a duty to help the police.'

'I've a duty to help a copper who's being bashed in the street, I agree,' Hugh said. 'But I can't see that I've a duty to take part in a far-fetched scheme that I've no faith in... And anyway, I've far too much to do.'

There was a little silence. Then Trant tried again. 'Well, we obviously don't see eye to eye on the plan – but I've a lot of experience of these things and I'd have thought that, up to a point, you'd have accepted my professional judgement... We really do need you, Mr Freeman. Believe me, your presence could make all the difference to the operation... Even if you're sceptical, I can't see why you should refuse. You're an unattached man, with no commitments...'

'I've a contract to write a book,' Hugh said.

'Oh, I appreciate that you're concerned about your writing – but that needn't be an obstacle. Where we're going, you should be able to carry on with your work very much as usual.'

For the first time, Hugh showed a flicker of interest. 'Where *would* we be going?'

'To an old tide mill on an Essex estuary. I'd prefer not to go into details at this stage – but I can assure you it will be a very quiet place.'

'I thought you expected gunfire!'

'I do – at some stage. But you don't, Mr Freeman. You can't have it both ways.'

Hugh laughed. 'Well, I must say the proposition sounds a bit more appealing now ... Would I have my own room?'

'Certainly.'

'Leisure to write?'

'Any amount of it.'

'Free board and lodging?'

'Of course.'

'Would I be able to move around?'

'Yes, quite a lot.'

'I see ...' Hugh considered. 'All right,' he said, 'I've changed my mind. I'll come for the ride.'

Trant looked relieved. 'I'm extremely obliged to you, Mr Freeman ... Now I think Miss Sheldon had better meet her stand-in. Will you tell them we're ready, Sergeant?'

A uniformed woman police sergeant came in first, followed closely by a girl. Trant introduced them. 'This is Sergeant Mellor – she'll be helping with the hair and the make-up ... This is our stand-in, Constable Lake ... Miss Sheldon, Mr Freeman. You'll be seeing a lot more of Mr Freeman, Constable, in the next week or two ...'

The girl said, 'Yes, sir,' and smiled at Hugh.

Debbie looked hard at her. She was in plain clothes – but they were the only plain thing about her. She had thick, dark hair like Debbie's own, a good figure, a beautiful complexion, and a charming smile. She was very pretty indeed. Like Debbie, she wore no ring.

'Well, let's see the two of you side by side,' Trant said. He lined them up and stood back, studying them. 'Yes – Constable Lake's a trifle taller, but I daresay that won't be noticed at a distance...' He didn't seem entirely satisfied. 'The hair's going to be the most important thing. Perhaps first of all we ought to have a photograph of Miss Sheldon...'

Debbie suddenly broke in. 'Can I say something, Superintendent?'

'Of course.'

'I'm not quite clear why you need a stand-in. Why can't I do the job myself?'

'Well...' Trant began – and paused.

'I'd much sooner be in it with everyone else,' Debbie said. 'It's not going to be much fun for me, twiddling my thumbs on my own for weeks ... Anyway, it's all so unnecessary ... Look at the trouble it's going to be, making Miss Lake up to look like me. And if it doesn't come off, the whole plan will fall through ... If you really want these men to believe I'm at the mill, or wherever, surely the best way is for me to *be* there.'

'That's true, of course...'

'Then what's the objection? Are you worried about the danger?'

'No,' Trant said, 'I'm not. Under the arrangements I'm making, there'd be virtually no danger as far as you were concerned – I think I could guarantee that. The reason I decided on a stand-in was that I thought you'd already had a great deal to put up with, and oughtn't to be subjected to any more strain. Where we're going, there'll be a lot of strain...'

'There will be anywhere,' Debbie said. 'Particularly if I've no one to share it with.'

'There'll also be very tight discipline and a good deal of tedium. It'll be rather like an army before action. In the end, there'll probably be some rather unpleasant happenings. I didn't think it fair to ask you to take part in all this, since it wasn't absolutely necessary.'

72

'That was nice of you,' Debbie said. 'But I'd much sooner.'

'Well, of course, if you feel like volunteering...'

Debbie gave an emphatic nod. 'I do.'

'It would certainly make everything a lot easier. We wouldn't need to look for a place for you – and we'd be saved the double guard... And it would undoubtedly improve our chances ... Are you absolutely sure about this, Miss Sheldon?'

'Absolutely.'

'You realize that you'll be like a prisoner? In a place of your own, it might be possible to relax precautions a little, once the gang's attention was concentrated elsewhere – but at the mill you'll have almost no freedom. And once you're there, it won't be possible for you to change your mind – however much you dislike it. You'll have to see it through to the end.'

'I realize all that. You can rely on me.'

'H'm...' Trant considered. 'Have you anything to say about it, Mr Freeman?'

'I'm all for it,' Hugh said.

'Very well...' Trant turned to the policewoman. 'Thank you, Sergeant. Thank you, Constable. It looks as though we shan't be needing you after all. Sorry to disappoint you.'

'That's all right, sir,' Sergeant Mellor said. The girl smiled at Hugh, and followed her out.

Hugh said, 'Well, you'd better start taking cookery lessons, Debbie... We shan't want scrambled eggs every day.'

Chapter Seven

As far as Hugh and Debbie were concerned, the next two days were passed in a twilight of expectant inactivity. 'Certain small changes' – as Trant put it – were being carried out by Yard technicians at the place they were going to, and until these were finished they would have to stay on at the hotel. During that time, the superintendent fully maintained his stringent precautions. Neither of them was allowed to go out of doors, and almost their only conversation was with each other and with Trant on the telephone. An exception was a talk Debbie had with a police lawyer, who called to go over the evidence she would be giving when Clay came up before the magistrates. Otherwise, they were kept *incommunicado*. Urgent shopping was done by Sergeant Norris and a plain-clothes policewoman and the parcels were left with the hall porter. Sergeant Everett, never intrusive but always at hand, was reinforced on the second day by another watchdog.

Debbie accepted the restrictions and the waiting philosophically. This, after all, was only the beginning – the feeling of claustrophobia was bound to get worse later on, so she might as well accustom herself to it. With Trant's permission, she spent a little time writing to her agent and to all the clients to whom she had promised work, regretting that because of illness she was temporarily out of action. It seemed the simplest way. She wrote on plain paper, without giving an address, and the letters were posted by the police in a suburb of North London. She received no post herself, since Trant was adamant that no one at all should visit the studio – though he hinted that the ban might be lifted before long. He was working now in a mysterious way, disclosing as little as possible of his activities and intentions.

Hugh was less patient than Debbie. He chafed at not being able to get on with his writing, and tried hard to persuade Trant to let him slip down to the cottage and collect his notes and his typewriter – but without success. He complained in hyperbolic phrases of the stuffiness of the hotel, the richness of the food, and the lack of opportunity for exercise. Only in the evenings did his mood noticeably improve, when he could drink, dine, and dance with Debbie. The evenings, he found, were fun ...

The newspapers were still showing great interest in the

jewel robbery and its aftermath. They were silent about Clay's alleged part in the affair, now that he'd been charged, but they mentioned various police activities, including inquiries among the neighbours at Cambridge and a second interview with Clay's wife. Several of them ran topical feature articles – about previous robberies, about how stolen jewellery was disposed of, about a smuggling racket to Amsterdam. All of them carried an item reporting that the insurance assessors in the Anstey case had offered a reward of £30,000 for information leading to the recovery of the stolen property – though none of them said anything about the efforts that were being made to find it. No mention was made, in any paper that Hugh saw, of police suspicions that the jewels might have been buried in Epping Forest, or of the fact that the police had been searching there. When Hugh expressed surprise about this in the course of a brief telephone conversation with Trant, the superintendent said he'd deliberately kept quiet about it because the less the gang knew about the police line of thought, the less likely they'd be to suspect a possible trap when the moment came. He'd been worried, he said, that reporters might have discovered about the search, but happily they hadn't. Now, for the time being, it had been called off, to avoid further risk. Trant, quite obviously, was more interested in getting the gang than in getting the jewels.

One item of news he *had* allowed to leak out. There were short paragraphs in several papers, quoting no source, saying it was understood that the anonymous telephone caller had now come forward and was under police protection. Great precautions were being taken, the papers said, to ensure that she'd be able to appear in court, and the police were planning to move her hiding place from time to time as an additional safeguard ... On the following day there were longer stories – imprecise but dramatic accounts of how the woman caller had taken a photograph of the robbers, how she'd been hoaxed by bogus policemen, how she'd been chased by the gang in Sussex, and rescued by a passing motorist. As Trant said, the gang knew most of the facts anyway – and they'd expect the papers to say something. Secrecy would worry them – but publicity of the normal kind would lull them . . .

It wasn't until after dark on the evening of Wednesday that the next big move occurred. When it came, it was swift and decisive. Trant telephoned to say that Hugh and Debbie should pay their hotel bill and meet him at the front door at eight-thirty exactly. Hugh settled the accounts with cash that the superintendent had provided, and at half past eight on the dot Trant walked in. He took them at once to a blue Mini parked outside, bundled them into the back, and drove away.

For a while, he didn't speak. He seemed to be watching the road behind him as well as the road in front. Then, as they reached the quietness of the business quarter and the traffic thinned, he relaxed.

'Well, we're on our way,' he said.

·TWO

Chapter One

THE TIDE MILL rose, a tall, gaunt rectangle, from a waste of land and water that had no distinguishable features in the darkness. Trant unlocked the front door and switched on a light. Hugh and Debbie followed him in.

They found themselves at once in a square room of barn-like proportions and appearance. The beamed ceiling was almost out of sight. The walls and floors were of naked brick. There was some sort of ventilating hole very high up in one of the walls, but there were no windows. The room was bare of furniture except for two incongruous-looking basket chairs with two small tables beside them and a complicated arrangement of wires leading away from them. The only other exit from the room was by a flight of steep wooden stairs that went straight up immediately opposite the front door. The air smelt dank.

'Cosy!' Hugh said. 'We'll be all right here.'

'This is only the entrance hall, Mr Freeman...' Trant went to the foot of the stairs and called up. In a moment, two men appeared. One of them was Sergeant Norris, who greeted Hugh and Debbie like old friends. The other was introduced as Sergeant Leigh. He was a very tall, lean man of about forty with a bony head and face. He nodded, but didn't speak.

'Everything in order?' Trant asked Norris.

'Yes, sir. All according to plan.'

'Good ... Well, we'll start by showing Miss Sheldon and Mr Freeman round the establishment.'

Debbie said, 'If we're going to be here for weeks, Super-intendent, don't you think you'd better start calling me by my first name?'

Trant gave her a fleeting smile. 'Very well ... Up you go, Debbie.'

It was a different world upstairs. Turning left from the first floor landing, they entered a large sitting-room, carpeted overall in pale green Wilton and pleasantly furnished with settees and soft chairs, well-fitted bookcases, a shining mahogany table in a dining area, and attractive concealed lighting. There was one very large window, now covered by a heavy curtain. On a round table near the window there was a wooden box with a black panel and a switch, and above it a loud-speaker.

'That's an intercom set,' Trant said. 'There's a similar one in each room. Anyone who wants to address the company can press the switch wherever he happens to be and his voice will be heard through the whole building. It should save us a lot of stair-climbing.'

They moved on. Across the landing there was a spacious, well-equipped kitchen. Then more stairs led to a bathroom and two bedrooms. The room that had been allotted to Debbie was the larger and more comfortable of the two. It was over the sitting-room, Trant told her, and looked out in the same direction. Its window was also heavily draped. Hugh's room was on the opposite side of the landing. In addition to the usual bedroom furniture it had a table, a hard chair, and what looked like a new reading lamp with an adjustable top. Hugh gave a satisfied nod. 'Yes – this should do all right for me,' he said. For a moment, he stood listening. 'It's certainly quiet enough now ... When shall I be able to get my typewriter, Superintendent?'

'All in good time, Mr Freeman ... Everything will be arranged.'

They moved on again. From the small landing a staircase that was hardly more than a ladder led to a vast loft, with a tiny window like an arrow-slit cut in each wall. It contained three single beds, a suitcase or two, some unopened packing cases, a short-wave radio set, and various bits of junk.

'Our quarters,' Trant said. 'The radio's a stand-by in case

the gang cut our telephone wires...' He met Hugh's
sceptical glance with a marble eye. 'Apart from the garage,
and a store cupboard in the entrance hall, you've seen
everything now ... Right – let's go down to the sitting-room
and have a conference...'

The conference began as a monologue.

'First, let me tell you a little about this place,' Trant said,
when they were all settled. 'It was built some two hundred
years ago. In the old days it was used for milling the local
corn. It stands on a tidal creek and the mill wheel was
turned by the rising and falling of the tide – hence the
name. All the inside machinery has gone and what's outside is pretty well rusted solid now, but as you can see the
house itself has been restored and modernized. It's owned
by a relative of one of our Assistant Commissioners. The
relationship isn't known to the public, so there's no danger
of the gang associating the place with Scotland Yard. The
owner. Mr Edwards, uses it mainly for summer holidays, but
at the moment he's in Canada. In theory you've rented it
from him, Mr Freeman, for a few weeks. The gang will
expect some sort of cover story, and if you happen to get
talking to anyone in the village and questions are asked,
that's it. Your name is Forbes and you're on holiday here
with Debbie – Miss Johnson, that is – and a friend.'

'*One* friend?' Hugh said. 'There are five of us.'

'Quite so – I'll come to that in a moment... This house,
by the way, stands entirely by itself in the middle of saltings and water meadows. The only other buildings within a
radius of a mile are a couple of farmhouses, neither of them
visible from here. The nearest village is two miles away –
it's called Tolbury. I've got a six-inch map of the area, and
a chart of the estuary, for anyone who's interested.'

Trant paused. 'Now, as you know, the object of this
exercise is to get the gang to move against Debbie. Before
they do that they'll want to make quite sure the girl here *is*
Debbie, and they'll want a pretty good idea of the set-up at
the house. So I expect them to start by watching the place.

There may be just one watcher or they may all join in. One thing we can be sure of – they'll merge into their surroundings and look very innocent. A lot of visitors come to this creek in good weather – picnickers, campers, hikers, bird-watchers, wildfowlers – and many of them carry binoculars. So the gang won't have any problem. Naturally we mustn't do anything to impede them or give any sign that we think they may be around. Debbie will actively assist them by showing herself – in daylight only – at this big window. It looks out on the channel and the saltings, and the watchers will find they have an excellent viewpoint with good cover from a bend in the sea wall about three hundred yards away.'

Hugh raised an eyebrow. 'An academic question, I'm sure, Superintendent – but what's to prevent them taking a shot at her with a rifle?'

'Chiefly,' Trant said, 'the risk that they might miss. It's a fairly long shot – and they won't dare to expose themselves by coming much closer in the daytime. At night there'll be curtains over the window – it'll be Leigh's job to make sure that they're all drawn at dusk ... If they did miss, or merely wounded, with the first shot, we'd be alerted and they'd have lost their chance – and they'll know this ... However, just to be on the safe side, we've had armoured glass put in all the windows.'

'Ah ...! Very dramatic!'

Trant continued. 'Debbie, of course, won't leave the house at all once the operation has begun. She won't go down to the entrance hall without permission. Her quarters will be this room, the bathroom and kitchen, and her bedroom. Is that all right, Debbie?'

'What more could a girl ask?' Debbie said.

Norris smiled. Trant merely looked grim.

'Right ... Now for the next point. It's of vital importance that the gang should be made to believe we're relying for security mainly on the *secrecy* of the hideout, not on an exceptionally strong defence. If they believe that, they'll be expecting a walkover when they come, and they should be easy meat. We mustn't do anything to give them the impression that we're lying in wait for them. Our defence measures at the house mustn't appear extreme – there must be no suggestion of a fortress, or a large garrison. In fact, we can afford to let them see only one man on guard – and he'll be Sergeant Leigh. They'll consider one man a routine precaution – indeed, they'll expect it. So Leigh, subject to his duties, will be allowed some freedom of movement outside. Norris and I won't show ourselves at all – either out of doors or at windows – and we shall do nothing to give our presence away. We shan't, for instance, answer the telephone ourselves ... We're both quite certain we weren't seen coming here. Norris was set down some miles away and finished the journey on foot after dark. I'm satisfied that no one followed us tonight. As far as the world's concerned, we're not here ... So you see, Mr Freeman, why I said *one* friend.'

Hugh nodded. 'And the Mini out there will be presumed to belong to Leigh?'

'That's right.'

'What are the arrangements for me?'

'You're in no danger from the gang on your own, so you'll be able to move around freely, as I promised. In fact, you'll be our leg man. If there's any reconnaissance to be done, you'll do it. Anything that's wanted, you'll get. Among other things, you'll be doing most of the shopping ... All strictly non-combatant duties.'

'It suits me,' Hugh said. 'I don't mind being the dogs-body.'

'Good ... Well, now we come to the serious part of the business – the likely tactics of the gang, and our own reply. I'll deal first with the possibility of a night assault, since that's much more likely than an attack in daylight. Some time after dark, and almost certainly at a very late hour when there's no one about, they'll converge upon the house. They may come along the sea wall, or over the saltings, or across the meadows, or along the road. From our point of view, it doesn't matter. We're not concerned with how they get here. Our defence point is the house.'

'No shooting till you see the whites of their eyes,' Hugh said.

'Exactly... Now what form will the attack take? Well, one great advantage of this place as a strong point is that it has only one outside door and no windows accessible from the ground – so if they want to get in, they'll have to use the front door. They can either knock and wait for the door to be opened, or they can break it down, or they can enter silently. Either of the first two would obviously bring an armed and alerted guard to the door – Leigh, whom they'll already have seen patrolling outside – and one of them might get hurt before the guard was disposed of. I'd expect, therefore, that they'd enter quietly. They'd have no difficulty about that. The lock's a simple one – I've deliberately kept it simple – and these men are experts at entering premises quickly and without noise. There are no bolts – as they can easily discover for themselves by listening from some near by point at lock-up time... So they'd slip in – probably all three of them – take the guard by surprise, and do what they'd come for... That, at least, would be my plan in their position...'

Trant paused for a comment, but none came. The policeman had heard his appreciation before. Debbie was looking a bit alarmed, Hugh more than a bit sardonic.

'All right,' Trant said. 'Now for the defence measures. If you'll come downstairs, there are a few gadgets I'd like to show you...'

They all trooped down. Trant went to the front door and opened it. 'First,' he said, 'there's our early-warning system... Outside here, under the gravel, we've installed a pattern of electric strips. When anyone approaches the door, a contact is made, and a buzzer sounds in the entrance hall. Like this...'

He pressed his foot on the gravel and there was a low buzz in the hall. 'From the outside,' he said, 'it's inaudible. We've tested it.'

He closed the door. 'Now in here we have two chairs. The

watch chairs. Through the hours of darkness, I shall occupy one, and Norris the other. The chairs have been carefully sited. One of them, as you see, is exactly opposite the front door. The other is a little to one side and covers the opening as the door swings back.'

He motioned Norris to one of the chairs and took the other himself. 'We'll say it's just after midnight. We're both sitting here, and of course we're both armed. The overhead light is on in the room – but as the front door has no glass in it and no cracks, the light can't be seen from outside. Suddenly, the buzzer sounds. I switch the light off from my chair, like this.' The light went out – and came on again. 'As you see, our electricians have been busy ... So now, we'll suppose, everything's dark. Our presence isn't suspected. We hear someone working on the lock of the door. Slowly, it creaks open. We hear footsteps advancing into the room. At that moment, I press another button ...'

The area around the front door was suddenly illuminated by a powerful beam of light from a lamp fixed at eye level near the bottom of the stairs.

'At once,' Trant said, 'the gang are caught in the spotlight. They're dazzled and can't see us – but we can see them perfectly. If they're carrying guns – and they probably will be – we open fire. If not, we call on them to surrender. By that time, Leigh will also be at hand – the buzzer sounds by his bed in the loft and he'll be standing by at the head of the stairs ... We should be well able to take care of things – but as a precaution against any unforeseen emergency, that phone over there gives us a direct line to a local headquarters and speedy reinforcement ... And that, I think, just about covers the night situation.'

'Very impressive,' Hugh said. 'It would look fine on the telly. Lights flashing, guns popping ...'

'This is going to be real, Mr Freeman.'

'H'm ... Anyhow, you certainly seem to have it all taped ... Provided, of course, that the gang are obliging enough to do things the way you expect.'

'Can you suggest any other way?'

'Well, as you know, I doubt if they'll come at all... If they do, I wouldn't bank on them following your rule book. Destiny comes sideways, didn't someone say? They've shown themselves to be resourceful blokes – they ought to be able to think of something a bit less direct.'

'Like what? Give me a practical alternative.'

'How about running a ladder up to Debbie's window? *We* know there's armoured glass there – but they don't.'

'We'd hear them,' Trant said. 'I should have mentioned that I've had concealed microphones fitted at intervals round the outside of the house. They'll be switched on at dusk and all sounds will register in the entrance hall – so we'll be completely safeguarded against any surprise development of that kind.'

'Fascinating...! But if the gang don't know about the mikes, they might try... What happens if they do?'

'Naturally, if we hear any suspicious sounds, we shall investigate – in the first place from the loft windows, which give an excellent view all round the foot of the house. But I don't think there'll be any sounds. These men will reject anything that involves protracted activity near the building, anything that means bringing up material or equipment, anything that could possibly give warning of their presence before they're ready to strike. They'll know that once we're alerted, we're likely to call up help right away. Whatever they do must be quick, sharp, and certain. That's why I say they'll make a direct attack with guns... However – any more suggestions?'

'What's the water supply here?' Hugh asked.

'It's pumped from a well in the meadow to a big tank above the loft. The pumping engine's in the garage.'

'Is the well out of range of the mikes?'

'Oh, yes...'

'Then what's to prevent them creeping up at night and shoving prussic acid in the well?'

'You're not serious, Mr Freeman?'

'Why not? They've done some pretty extravagant things already.'

'First they'd have to find the well,' Trant said. 'In the dark . . . Then they'd have to make certain the concentration was going to be lethal when it reached us – which I doubt if they could do . . . But more important, they'd have to make sure Debbie was the first victim – otherwise it would be like missing with the first rifle shot. And they couldn't make sure.'

'That's true . . . Well, let's think – there must be plenty of unorthodox ways of attacking a place . . .' Hugh grinned. 'What about balloon bombs? I seem to remember the Austrians used them against Cavour's Venice when it was under siege.'

'Oh, yes . . .? What happened?'

'As a matter of fact, they fell on their own ships . . .'

'I'm not surprised . . . Well, I don't propose to take any precautions against balloons . . . Any further observations, Mr Freeman?'

'Only that I still think you may be underrating the ingenuity of these men,' Hugh said. 'But I'm bound to admit I can't think of an alternative method off-hand.'

'Then I'll wind up with just a word on the possibility of a daylight attack. It's obviously very slight, because there's an open view all round the house and no one can approach the place without being seen – but we'd better not rule it out entirely. I'll tell you the daytime dispositions. For much of the day, Norris and I will be up in the loft, doing shifts. One of us will be sleeping – the other will be keeping a lookout from the loft windows. Leigh will be down here in the entrance hall or patrolling outside. At the first sign of anything potentially dangerous or suspicious, the three of us will join up here and I shall take charge.'

Hugh grunted. 'As a matter of interest what would you do if – say – three men and a woman came rowing up the creek in a dinghy and tied up here and knocked at the door?'

'Well, actually that particular thing couldn't happen,' Trant said, 'because there's a footbridge across the creek lower down and nothing can get through . . . But in general the policy will be to keep the door shut if we see any strangers approaching in a bunch or converging on us. That way we can't go wrong ... However, I don't expect any strangers to call. There'll be no post for any of us, no deliveries by tradesmen, no reason for visitors ... My guess is that our days won't be disturbed at all.'

'Now there I'm with you,' Hugh said.

There was a little pause. Then Trant continued, 'There's just one other thing. If an attack's going to come, I'd expect it to come sooner rather than later. The gang must be impatient to get the jewels back in their hands – they can't be happy at leaving half a million pounds lying around in a forest. And if once Clay is sent for trial, it'll be many weeks before they can hope to see him. So I think they'll strike before the committal date. That means that with luck our stay here will be shorter than you feared, Debbie. It also means that we'll have to be on our toes from the start ... Now – any more questions?'

'Only the obvious one,' Hugh said. 'How are the gang going to find out where the hide-out is?'

'That, Mr Freeman, is where you come into the picture again ... I suggest we go upstairs and make ourselves comfortable and I'll tell you the plan over a glass of beer.'

Leigh and Norris carried the beer up from the store cupboard. Hugh fetched tumblers from the kitchen. Trant showed Debbie into one of the soft chairs and took the one beside her. The two sergeants occupied the settee. Hugh seated himself at the table, a little apart from the others, as though to emphasize his dissident views.

'Right,' Trant said, 'here's how I see the situation ... From the moment the gang lost track of Debbie, they must have had only one idea – to find her again. Now how would they have set about it? Well, I know what I'd have been doing in their position. I'd have tried to keep a continuous watch on her studio – and my guess is that that's exactly what they've been doing. They know that all Debbie's belongings are there, and that if she's going to be holed up somewhere for several weeks she's bound to want some of them. They can't hope she'll be allowed to fetch them herself, but they'll expect someone to show up some time. And when someone does, they'll try to follow him. It was because of that possibility that I wouldn't let anyone go back there before. Now it's a situation we can use.'

'Assuming your guess is right,' Hugh said.

'Of course . . . Now another possibility is that one of them may have been watching your cottage, Mr Freeman. After the chase it must have seemed well on the cards that you'd go with Debbie to the police – and perhaps get involved in the case – so they'd certainly have had an interest in you . . . I don't suppose they'd have had any difficulty in tracing your new address.'

'I shouldn't think so. I told a couple of neighbours in Brighton where I was going.'

Trant nodded. 'And if they *have* been keeping an eye on the cottage, they'll know you haven't been back since the weekend – and that will have increased their interest. Someone may very well be hanging about there until you return – again, with the idea of being led to Debbie.'

'I get it,' Hugh said. 'I'm to dash around being a decoy.'

'That's right . . . Early tomorrow morning, Leigh will drive you into Colchester and you'll get a train to London. You'll pick up your car at the Yard and drive to your cottage. There, you'll collect the things that you're likely to need here, including your typewriter. You'll drive at a steady pace back to London, park outside the studio or as near to it as you can get, and collect the things that Debbie needs. She'll make out a list for you. Then you'll drive back here, again at a steady pace. With a car like yours, anyone who wants to follow you will have no trouble.'

'They could do it by ear!' Hugh said.

'I imagine so . . . Of course, I need hardly emphasize how important it is that the gang shouldn't suspect they're being led on. You must try to behave all the time in an unconcerned way – and above all, avoid showing any interest in what's behind you when you're driving.'

'That's not what the Highway Code says.'

'Never mind that... Now if anything should delay you so that you can't get back in daylight, don't come at all – give me a ring instead. The number's Tolbury 4488. The gang will hardly be set for an attack right away – but we'll take no chances in the dark until we're ready... One final point. When you reach Tolbury village on your way back, stop for a few moments. If the shops are still open, buy something. If they're not, get out and look at a tyre. Then drive on slowly. The road from the village to here is a private one and it's clearly marked – "Private Road – Tide Mill Only". What we want is for anyone following you to note the sign but not to continue along the road – otherwise we may end up with a premature confrontation. He won't want that, either. So give him plenty of opportunity to read the notice... And that's it... All clear, Mr Freeman?'

'Clear as moonshine, Superintendent. You're certainly an optimist... Suppose I'm not followed? Suppose nothing at all happens? What then?'

'Then we'll have to try something else,' Trant said.

The time was ten o'clock. The policemen had gone upstairs to unpack their crates, leaving Hugh and Debbie alone. Debbie was working on the list of things she wanted brought from the studio.

Hugh said, 'What do you think of our Supremo?'

Debbie looked up, pencil poised. 'He's impressive, isn't he? Rather terrific really.'

'A bit overbearing, wouldn't you say?'

'Well – he is the man in charge.'

'Humourless?'

'Not really... I think he's weighed down by his responsibilities.'

'Long-winded?'

'Not more than he has to be... I thought he was quite brief this evening, considering how much he had to tell us.'

'Over-confident?'

'Perhaps covering up uncertainty . . . Who can tell?'

Hugh grunted. 'I gather you find him sympathetic.'

'I think I might, when I got to know him better.'

'H'm . . . He liked you, that's obvious. But he doesn't approve of me at all. I guess we're just antagonistic types. I hate discipline and authority, and he knows it. He'd like nothing better than to put me on a charge, if he could.'

'Well, you do rather needle him.'

'I can't help it – he's so damned sure about everything . . . What am I supposed to do – pretend to agree with him when I don't? All this tomfoolery . . . I can see myself having a flaming row with him before we're through.'

'Don't do that, for heaven's sake. It would make life unbearable.'

'I know – but he does get under my skin . . . Oh, well . . . How's the list going?'

'It's almost finished,' Debbie said. 'One more item . . . Do you think you'll be able to get my easel into the car? It folds up, but not very small, I'm afraid.'

'What easel?'

'For painting . . . And my bag of painting things? They're in one of the studio cupboards.'

'Oh, you paint, do you?'

'Only as a hobby. And not often – I don't get the chance. But it should be a good opportunity down here.'

'Well, I'll have a bash,' Hugh said. He took the list from her, glanced down it, and whistled. 'Moving house, eh? You didn't tell me.'

'Don't be horrid . . . I know it looks a lot, but if I'm going to be here for weeks I must have a few clothes and books and things.'

'That's all right,' Hugh said. 'My middle name's Pickford . . .' He looked at the list again, pretended to weigh it in his hand, and put it in his pocket. 'It shouldn't take me more than about a fortnight . . . !'

Chapter Two

DEBBIE HAD drawn back her curtains before going to bed and the morning light woke her soon after seven. She put on her dressing-gown and went to the window. The sky was clear, the sun was shining, the outlook over the saltings and the estuary enchanting. She dressed quickly, crossed the landing, and knocked on Hugh's door. He was shaving.

'Good morning,' she said. 'How about coming for a stroll before breakfast? It's a gorgeous day and the view's marvellous.'

'Aren't you on the ball and chain yet?'

'Not till you get back this evening... Come on, it's our one chance to look round together.'

'Okay,' Hugh said. 'I'll be ready in ten minutes.'

'I'll see you outside, then...' Debbie went downstairs and let herself out. The air had a strong, seaweedy tang. She took a deep, satisfying breath and gazed around. There was a paved forecourt in front of the mill, with a patch of flower garden and a rustic seat. She sat down in the sun, warming herself and looking up at the house, till Hugh joined her.

'It's an interesting building,' she said. 'Hardly a thing of beauty, though, is it?'

Hugh considered. 'No – it's a bit of an eyesore, actually...' The proportions of the mill were functional rather than pleasing. The windowless front gave it a blind, shut-in look. The weather-boarding that covered most of its brickwork was dry and cracked and badly in need of attention. Some of the boards were hanging loose and looked as though they might fall away at any moment. The structure was built into, and formed part of, an otherwise continuous sea wall, and on the seaward side its lower surface was covered with slimy green weed where the high tides had lapped against it. The general appearance of the place wasn't improved by a copse of ancient conifers, now little more than a tangle of dead wood, that pressed and scraped against the western corner of the building.

'It looks as though the owner lost interest when he'd done up the inside,' Debbie said.

Hugh nodded. 'Or else he ran out of cash – it must cost a fortune to keep up a place like this... Let's see what the surroundings look like from the top of the wall.'

Debbie ran ahead of him up the sloping bank beside the house. 'It's lovely,' she cried. Hugh joined her, and together they gazed around. The vista was fascinating. All about them was space and flatness, under an enormous Constable sky. The horizon formed an almost perfect circle, broken only by a few clumps of elms and slanting poplars. The sea wall, its arms stretching away on either hand and then converging again, enclosed a peninsula of tide-washed land that opened out again northwards from a narrow neck. Within the walls the expanse of grey-green saltings was scored by a deep channel running through its centre. At present there was only a trickle of water in the channel and its steep, muddy sides glistened yellow in the early sun. From the main creek, innumerable side rills cut a tracery through the saltings like the veins of a hand. Debbie pointed out the bend in the left-hand sea wall three hundred yards away which Trant had mentioned as a possible viewpoint for the gang. Close beside it was the footbridge he'd spoken of. In the far distance, away towards the sea, the bare poles of sailing boats showed against the sky.

'I suppose it all gets completely covered when the tide's high,' Debbie said.

'Yes, it'll be like a lake. Right up to the walls.'

'That'll be a sight... But it looks beautiful now. Such lovely shapes... And the colours are so restful.'

'Isn't it the same view that you see from your window?'

'Yes,' she said. 'I shall try to paint it.'

They turned and looked in the opposite direction. On the landward side of the wall the view was quite different but no less satisfying. There were green water-meadows, dotted with small trees, drained by freshwater dykes and grazed by cows. To the east of the house, the meadows formed only a

91

narrow belt between the sea wall and what appeared to be a new, embanked road. To the west, they stretched tranquilly to the horizon. It was a peaceful and a beckoning scene.

Hugh could imagine himself walking happily here for hours.

Presently they left the wall and strolled round to what had been the working end of the mill, where the creek passed by on its way inland. The power of the tides had been confined here to a narrow, brick-lined channel, spanned by an iron bridge and closed to everything but water by the huge, now derelict mill wheel. Above the mill the creek continued – still walled on both sides – for some hundreds of yards. Then it widened into a shallow basin, its further course blocked by the built-up road.

They were standing on the bridge, watching two belligerent green crabs clashing their claws together in the mud, when there was a loud halloo from the front of the house.

'The voice of the workhouse master,' Hugh said, with a grin. 'We'd better go in and have our skilly.'

Immediately after breakfast Hugh left for Colchester station with Sergeant Leigh. He was just in time to catch a fast train for London, reached Liverpool Street at eleven, took a taxi to the Yard, picked up the Vauxhall, and set off for the cottage, driving as fast as the heavy traffic permitted.

A night's reflection had made him even more doubtful about Trant's decoy hopes. Apart from anything else, it seemed to him that watching the studio – let alone the cottage – would have been too much for the gang's man-power resources. To be worth while, any watch would have had to continue right round the clock – and he thought it unlikely that three men could have kept that up, day after day. Of course, they might have had women around to help – Clay's wife, for instance. But it all seemed most improbable . . . Not that Hugh had any objection to the trip. He'd have had to make it anyway, to collect his belongings and

Debbie's – or someone would. And it was no hardship, driving around in his open jalopy on a fine day.

He reached the cottage shortly after one. There was a small grey van parked on the grass verge just below the house, with a man behind the wheel eating his lunch. For a moment, Hugh wondered. The van had no markings on it – and he'd never known anything stop there before. But the man seemed to take no interest in him … The cottage itself was just as he and Debbie had left it. He spent a few minutes getting himself a quick snack out of tins. Then he gathered together the things he'd need at the mill – his typewriter, tape recorder and record player, his manuscript, a few reams of paper, some books and notes, clothes, gumboots, and an electric handlamp – and stowed them in the back of the car. By two o'clock he was ready to leave.

It was when he slowed for the main road that he noticed the grey van coming up behind him. It must have left the lane at the same time that he did. He turned right towards London – and the van turned too. It *did* seem to be following him. The road was congested with summer holiday-makers and the van was stuck in the queue, several cars behind, but keeping up. Hugh's instinct was to press ahead and throw it off – or stop and let it pass. Reluctantly – and uneasily – he obeyed Trant's instructions and continued at a steady pace. He kept glancing in his mirror – he couldn't help it … Then, at traffic lights in Lewes, he saw the van turn off. It had all been imagination …

He reached the studio at four o'clock, a little behind his planned schedule. He managed to find a space to park, climbed the stairs, and let himself in with Debbie's key. It was an odd feeling, being there on his own as though he were some old and trusted friend – when four days before, he hadn't even met her. He walked through the apartment, taking in its exquisite neatness, admiring the Chinese ducks in the sitting-room, interested in the workman-like appointments in the studio – conscious above all, and pleasantly, of the trace of scent in the air. Then he got to work on Debbie's formidable list. It was detailed and methodical, with many of the items precisely described and their where-abouts indicated. He started to pile things on the divan bed – clothes and shoes, bottles and boxes from a foldaway dressing-table, brush and comb, books from the shelves, camera and films, packets of chemicals and processing dishes from the studio, a huge pad of drawing paper, transistor radio, diary, cookery book, letters from the mat. When he'd reached the end of the list he packed two large suitcases and carried them down to the car. He had to return three times for loose items that wouldn't go in the cases, and once more for the easel and the paint bag. Then he locked up, squeezed himself into the laden car, and drove slowly away.

The roads were busier than ever now – with home-going commuter traffic, as well as holidaymakers. All through the City, all along Commercial Road, all up Eastern Avenue, all along the A-12, he was in a bonnet-to-tail stream. September 5th, he thought – and the congestion was as bad as in high summer. Even when he turned off the A-12 towards the sea, on what was supposed to be a minor road, there were cars strung out behind him at thirty-yard intervals. At least four or five were visible in his mirror when he drove into the square in Tolbury village.

He stopped there, as Trant had instructed him. It was half past six and the shops were shut – but the pubs were open. He parked in the square and went into a pub called the Anchor and had a much-needed pint. He emerged just before seven, stood for a moment by the car, nonchalantly filling his pipe, and then without hurrying took the road signposted 'Tide Mill Only'. Now, for the first time, there were no cars behind him and he could say positively that he was not being followed. But he felt pretty convinced that no one had bothered about him at any stage of the journey.

Trant came out to meet him as he drove into the fore-court. 'Nicely timed, Mr Freeman – I was just beginning to wonder about you ... Well, have you anything to report?'

'Not a thing,' Hugh said. 'Except that it's been a long, hard day.'

While Norris and Leigh helped him to unload the car and carry the things upstairs, Debbie had a few words with Trant about the domestic arrangements at the mill, now that the garrison were about to go over to their defence routine. Nobody had actually asked her to take charge of the housekeeping, but everyone seemed to assume that she would – which was reasonable enough. But there were problems.

'It's a question of organizing the meals,' she said. 'We'll have to have them in shifts, shan't we?'

'I suppose we will,' Trant said. It was one of the few matters he'd given no thought to.

Debbie produced a slip of paper. 'I've tried to work something out ... You and Sergeant Norris will be finishing your downstairs watch at daylight, didn't you say? About seven o'clock?'

'That's right.'

'Well, how about you two having your breakfast straight away before you go upstairs? I expect you'll be ready for it ... Sergeant Leigh would be up by then, so he could be watching from the loft while you ate ... Then he could come down and have his breakfast with Hugh and me before he started his duties outside.'

'Excellent,' Trant said.

'Now about lunch – wouldn't it be better to make that portable snacks, so that everyone could have it where they happened to be? Cold snacks, I should think – then whoever's sleeping wouldn't have to be wakened.'

'Yes – that'll do splendidly.'

'And dinner will have to be in shifts again ... What time will you and Sergeant Norris be starting your night watch?'

'About eight-thirty.'

'Then you two had better eat first – at half past seven.'

Trant nodded. 'While Leigh's still on watch.'

'Then he can join Hugh and myself again ... I think that's all right.'

'It sounds most efficient,' Trant said. 'I'm afraid it's going to mean a lot more trouble for you, though.'

95

'No trouble at all,' Debbie said. She smiled. 'I shall endeavour to give satisfaction, sir, in my new post.'

Supper that evening was a scratch affair from stores that Trant had laid in. Then, as dusk fell, the planned defensive measures went into operation. Trant reminded Debbie that from now on she must confine herself to the upper floors. Sergeant Leigh did a round of the windows, carefully drawing all the curtains. Norris switched on the outside microphones and checked that the buzzers and spotlight were working properly. Then he and Trant donned thick sweaters and soft-soled shoes and took up their positions in the entrance hall.

When Hugh went down around nine o'clock to see what was going on, he found them reading magazines and looking pretty comfortable in their basket chairs. On the tables were bottles of beer, and sandwiches that Debbie had made for them. On the ground beside each of them there was a short, ugly-looking gun with a shoulder sling.

Hugh stared at the guns. 'What on earth are those things?'

'Belgian FN rifles,' Trant told him. 'Army type ... They fire two hundred rounds a minute on automatic.'

'Good lord ...! That's going a bit far, isn't it?'

'I don't think so, Mr Freeman. It's no good relying on cavalry when the other side may have armoured columns.'

'You don't seriously think the gang might turn up with guns like that?'

'I wouldn't be at all surprised.'

'Incredible!' Hugh said.

He went to his room to get his manuscript. Then he joined Debbie in the sitting-room. 'I've just been inspecting the battle stations,' he said. 'Honestly, it's out of this world. They're armed to the teeth – got everything except tin hats ....!'

'I expect they know what they're doing," Debbie said. She

glanced at the papers Hugh was holding. 'What have you got there? – the opus?'

'Yes ... I wondered if you'd care to have a look at it – as far as it's gone.'

'I'd love to,' she said. She took the sheaf of typescript and at once began to read.

Hugh lit his pipe and sat watching her. She looked charming, he thought, curled up on the settee, with her dark hair flung back over one shoulder and her face eager and intent.

There were only forty pages and she read fast. Hugh waited anxiously for her comment as she reached the end.

'It's jolly good,' she said. 'I don't know what you're worrying about.'

'Honestly?'

'Cross my heart...! It moves fast, and the characters talk like real people, and the background's fascinating... Now I can't wait to read the rest.'

Hugh gave a pleased smile. 'In that case, I'll finish it!' he said.

In the morning, Hugh drove into the village with a sizeable shopping list from Debbie and a wad of notes provided by Trant. He was buying, the superintendent had reminded him, daily provisions for a notional three people, so he mustn't too obviously be buying for five or someone might start getting ideas. A little care in spreading his purchases covered that. The village facilities were limited, but inside an hour he'd managed to get most of the things on the list, or some adequate substitute. The only thing he bought that wasn't on the list was a large bunch of michaelmas daisies – which, ten minutes later, he presented to Debbie.

'I thought that Trant would like me to get them,' he said, straightfaced. 'After all, you're supposed to be on holiday with me in some capacity – so I probably would bring you flowers... It's important to give the right impression in the village.'

'They're gorgeous,' Debbie said. 'Thank you . . . They'll brighten the place up wonderfully.'

Hugh hung around. 'Anything I can do . . .?'

'Not really . . . Everything's under control.'

He nodded. 'Then I think I'll take a short stroll before I get down to work . . . See you later.'

He went first along the sea wall to the right. The sun was warm, the air sweet with the scent of out-of-season hay. Someone, he noticed, had recently cut the long grass on the landward slope of the wall and piled it up in a rough stack beside the conifers. Just beyond, there was a stile and a rutted track leading off across the meadows. A family party were approaching along it, laden with picnic things. Hugh smiled and nodded to them as he passed. He was in a lighthearted mood· this morning. He'd slept well, the day was perfect for a walk, Debbie had been encouraging about his story, and the only danger he foresaw was that Trant and Norris would accidentally shoot each other! He felt on top of the world.

He stopped for a moment at the viewpoint and glanced back towards the mill. He could see Debbie at the sitting-room window, carrying out Trant's instructions to show herself. She had set up her easel and was painting. Hugh waved to her, and she saw him and waved back.

He edged past a couple of black-and-white Friesians that blocked his path and walked on, eager to see what lay behind the next curve of the wall – and the next. He paused to look at the skeleton timbers of a boat beached long ago; to note a long, grey duck-punt tucked away in a rill; to examine a sea plant; to wonder what depths of mud lay under those carpets of mossy yellow in the saltings. He tried to spot a skylark that was trilling away in the blue. He stood and watched as a pair of swans flew over with creak-ing wings and necks outstretched. There was really nothing, he thought, to equal a sea wall for a walk. Every sight and sound was pleasing. With no cars to bother about, you could stride on for miles, unmolested and secure. Secure, that is, if you kept an eye open for the occasional deep hole or concealed obstruction in the grass-covered clay surface of the wall. Even here, a man could break a leg.

He strolled on for half an hour, meeting no one. Presently he came in sight of the two farmhouses Trant had spoken of. He turned there, and began slowly to retrace his steps. With no fresh discoveries to make, he sank gradually into thought, planning the next stage of his story.

It wasn't until he reached the viewpoint again that he returned to the real world. There was a path across the neck of the saltings by way of the wooden footbridge – a useful short cut to the opposite wall. He slid down the sloping concrete blocks that formed the sea defence on the saltings side and squelched along the path to the bridge. It was a rickety affair, of a handrail and two lines of planks, set up on slender wooden piles. The piles had been driven into the muddy bed of the channel at intervals of a couple of feet and, as Trant had said, they virtually closed the creek. Hugh stood there for a while, watching the tide flowing in. The water was an opaque greyish-brown, with a bubbly froth, and it flowed fast between the steep, symmetrically-angled mud banks of the channel. Its surface was littered with debris, mostly weed and small bits of wood, which collected against the bridge and stayed there. Hugh watched a piece of timber drifting slowly up towards him, sometimes sticking a little on the mud at the edge of the water, but always being washed off in the end and carried on. Presently, by some trick of the current, it was deflected out of the channel and up one of the tributary rills. These were less deep than the main channel and were only just beginning to fill. There was one particularly large one, named Smallgains on the map, that forked away above the bridge in a southeasterly direction. Its banks of mud looked incredibly glutinous. Hugh put a foot down experimentally and almost lost a gumboot. It came out finally with a sucking sound, leaving a deep hole in a substance that looked like black putty and smelt foul.

He continued along the path to the opposite wall. To his

left, now, and not far away, were the masts of the small boats that he'd seen from the house. He made a mental note that there must be some sort of anchorage there and that it would be an interesting place to look over on some other occasion. Today, he turned to the right, back towards the mill. A hundred and fifty yards from the house there was another bend in the wall, sharper than the one at the viewpoint. Enclosed by the bend there was a patch of shingly beach – a popular spot with visitors, judging by the litter that had been left lying about. Near by, a big rill ended at the wall. Hugh identified it as the southern end of Smallgains. Where it met the wall there was a sluice – a round metal door with a concrete ledge over it, designed to let landwater drain to the saltings and keep the sea water off the land. On the landward side there was a weedy dyke parallel to the wall, with a plank across it and another footpath leading to the built-up road.

Hugh stood for a moment, gazing around. It was, he thought, a fascinating scene, with the tide flowing and the rills filling and the shape of everything constantly changing. There was motion – yet there was peace... With a sense of deep satisfaction, he completed the circuit to the mill.

Sergeant Leigh was pacing up and down the forecourt like a soldier on sentry-go. Each time he turned, he glanced across at the private approach road. Occasionally he climbed the sea wall and looked around before resuming his beat.

Hugh acknowledged his friendly salute. 'Not much doing, eh, Sarge?'

'Not at the moment, sir.'

Hugh walked over to the Vauxhall. Its wire wheels were coated with dried mud and its paintwork was filthy. 'I suppose there isn't a hose anywhere around, is there?'

'There's one in the garage, sir. And a tap by the wall there...' Leigh stopped pacing and came over. 'Going to give her a clean-up?'

'I think I will.'

Leigh ran a hand along the Vauxhall's fluted radiator. 'She's a fine old car, isn't she? Got real character ... They don't make cars like her these days.'

'They certainly don't.'

'She's got leg room, too. In most cars, I'm scared I'm going to knock myself out with my knees...' Leigh went into the garage, hauled out the hose, joined it to the tap, and found a sponge. 'There you are, sir.'

'Thank you, Sarge.' Hugh shed his jacket and started to hose the car down. 'It must be pretty dull for you,' he said, 'holding the fort out here on your own with not an enemy in sight.'

'Oh, it's not too bad, sir – it's good exercise, and all in the day's work. Sometimes jobs are dull – sometimes they're not dull enough...! We take what comes.'

'Do you enjoy being a policeman?'

'Yes, it suits me fine... Plenty of variety – and a bit of status attached to the job ... Not that the public appreciate us the way they should – not till they really need us. Then they do...' Leigh strolled over to the wall, looked around, and came back. 'Of course, we need more chaps – we don't get our proper free time, that's the trouble. Almost always on duty, you might say.'

'Not much fun for your wife, eh?'

'Well, I'm not married yet, sir, so I wouldn't know ... Never seemed to meet the right kind of girl, somehow.'

Hugh gave an understanding nod. 'What about Trant and Norris – are they married?'

'Oh, yes... The Super's got a couple of grown-up boys – he started young... Norris was married last year.'

'Have you worked with Trant before?'

'Yes – a couple of times.'

'Bit of a martinet, isn't he?'

'You have to be on a job like this,' Leigh said. 'He's a fine policeman. He's got a great reputation at the Yard.'

'Rather unorthodox, wouldn't you say?'

'Oh, he's that, all right. His old man was the same – he

was a copper, too. He helped to start what they called the "ghost squad" in the last war – chaps that joined the underworld in disguise and then took part in criminal jobs. Pretty good idea, if you ask me – but the public wouldn't stand for it when the war was over ...' Leigh shook his head sadly over the public. 'You can't fight these villains with kid gloves – you've got to be smart and tough, and that's what the Super is. I'd sooner have him around in a tight spot than anyone I know.'

'You don't think *we're* going to be in a tight spot, do you?'

Leigh shrugged. 'It depends whether the gang find us or not. But I reckon they will. If it turns out they didn't follow you yesterday, the Super'll drop a hint somewhere ... There's always the underworld grapevine.'

'But do you think they'll attack the house if they do find us?'

'Why not, sir ...? Those bastards would shoot a place up if their own mother was in it – as long as there was dough to be had. And what have they got to lose? They've killed several people already, so now they can do it for free. If they killed a hundred more, they'd be no worse off. That's what no-hanging's done for us ... Yes, I reckon they'll attack, all right. So does Norris.'

'H'm – I'm in a minority of one, then ... Anyway, doesn't the prospect worry you?'

'Because of the danger, you mean?' Leigh shook his head. 'If your number's up, it's up. In our job, you've got to be philosophical.'

'I suppose so ...' Hugh gave the car bonnet a final rub down, and stood back. 'There, that's better.'

'Yes, she looks fine ... Don't bother about the hose, sir – I'll put it away.'

'Thanks,' Hugh said.

He found Debbie busy in the kitchen. She had a coloured handkerchief over her hair and a coloured apron round her waist and was cooking something in a very large saucepan.

Hugh sniffed. 'That smells good... Something for lunch?'

'No, it's not,' Debbie said severely. 'Lunches are cold, as you very well know... It's for dinner.'

'What is it?'

'Stew.'

'Anyone I know?'

'For that,' Debbie said, 'you shan't have any.'

Hugh sat down and watched her. 'You're looking very bright and cheerful this morning.'

'Good... I feel cheerful.'

'You know,' Hugh said, 'for a dedicated career girl you're not doing at all badly here.'

'Thank's... How's the life of Reilly?'

'If you ask me, you're a housewife *manqué*.'

'Not in the least... It's simply that someone's got to look after four helpless men.'

'I'm not helpless.'

'All right – three, then.'

'Oh, I don't mind having the odd meal cooked for me... It makes a pleasant change.'

'It makes a change for me, too, cooking them.'

'You're enjoying yourself, aren't you?'

'As a matter of fact, I am,' Debbie said. 'It's like a holiday... No telephone to answer, no post to catch, no jobs to finish, no rat race... Four strong men to make a fuss of me – three of them quite nice...'

Hugh grinned. 'Yes – it's a pity about Trant.'

'It's a pity about you...! When are you going to start work?'

'I've been working quite a bit this morning,' Hugh said. 'After my fashion... Even an oyster needs time to make its pearl.'

'Some oysters don't make pearls!'

'Anyway, I'm so exhausted I need a drink. How about me mixing a small knock-out drop for us?'

'It's a nice idea.'

Hugh got up. 'Right, I will ...' He turned at the door.

'To tell you the truth, I like being here, too. I'm glad I came.'

Immediately after lunch, Hugh retired to his room. He moved his table away from the window so that he couldn't be distracted by the view, put a new ribbon in his typewriter, arranged his paper and his notes, filled his pipe, and got down to work.

At first he was aware of strangeness. The table wasn't quite as solid as his own at the cottage. The arms of the chair weren't quite the right height. The typewriter seemed to make a different sound. The light came from a different angle. He wasn't sure he'd be able to settle down. Taking up the thread was always tricky, even in familiar surroundings... But at least the place was quiet. Not a sound came from the building, and hardly a sound from outside. Little by little, his concentration grew. It helped that he'd left his story at a point where it was interesting to start again. Soon he was completely absorbed in his imaginary world.

When, at the end of the chapter, he looked at his watch, he saw without surprise that it was nearly seven o'clock. Time always slipped by unnoticed when work was going well. Four hours solid... He got up stiffly and went down to stretch his legs before dinner.

The evening, like the day, passed peacefully. Having eaten, Trant and Norris took up their positions in the entrance hall at the usual time. The other three sat over their meal for a while, chatting. At ten, Debbie asked Leigh to take a final cup of tea down to the watchers. At eleven, there was a general retirement to bed. By midnight, the mill was wrapped in total silence.

It was some time in the early hours that Hugh was jerked out of sleep by a noise overhead. He listened. He could hear hurried footsteps, a movement on the stairs. Something was happening. He threw on his dressing-gown and went to the door. Leigh, fully clothed, was descending to the first landing. He had his automatic rifle slung over his shoulder.

'What's going on?' Hugh called. Leigh turned, his face tense, his finger to his lips. 'The buzzer's gone!' he said in a sibilant whisper.

Hugh joined him at the top of the first flight. The light was out in the hall but there was a glimmer from the upper landing and the shadowy figures of Trant and Norris were just visible. They were poised for action on the edge of their chairs, their guns pointed at the door. Through the mike came the sound of stealthy movements outside. Trant's left hand moved to the spotlight button. Hugh watched, incredulous, his pulse racing.

They waited, frozen in their postures. There was a scraping sound at the door ... Then the overhead light suddenly blazed on. 'All right,' Trant called, 'you can come down.'

Hugh followed Leigh to the hall. The watchers had relaxed. Norris was grinning sheepishly. From outside the door there was a new sound, quite unmistakable. A snuffling ... The exploratory snuffle of a dog on the prowl.

'Those electric strips are a bit *too* sensitive,' Trant said. 'Still, it was a useful bit of practice ... Next time, Leigh, make sure those upper lights are out.'

Leigh nodded. 'Yes, sir ... Sorry, sir.'

Hugh looked disgustedly at the three policemen. 'I think you're all nuts,' he said.

The next day was Saturday, which meant a double lot of shopping for the weekend. Hugh raced through it at top speed, dumped his purchases in the kitchen, and at once shut himself up in his room. His story had begun to flow freely, he was enjoying writing again, he'd nothing on his mind to disturb him, and working conditions were excellent. Better, he had to admit, than any he'd known. During his absence in the village, Debbie had cleaned up his room. She hadn't touched any of his papers, but she'd emptied the brimming ashtray and waste basket, swept the floor and put a few michaelmas daisies in a vase on the mantelpiece. Hugh himself had never bothered much about clearing the decks before he started work, but now someone else was doing it he welcomed it. It was pleasant, too, to think that there were no dirty dishes piling up in the sink – and that in three hours' time there'd be a tasty lunch snack waiting for him . . . This really *was* the life of Reilly . . . He lit his pipe and quickly took up the thread of his story . . .

At one o'clock, whistling a cheerful tune, he went down to the sitting-room for a pre-lunch martini. Debbie had just put the final touches to her picture and was standing back with her head on one side, appraising it.

'May I see?' Hugh asked.

'Of course . . .'

He joined her by the easel. The water colour showed the creek and saltings shortly after half tide. The delicate shades of the sea grass and the mud had been well caught.

'Nice,' he said. 'And not a crook in sight!'

'Oh – I painted them out.'

He laughed. 'I like it . . . Clever girl.'

'I don't think it's too bad myself.'

'What will you do with it – take it home and hang it?'

'I might . . . It'll be an interesting memento. And I've got really fond of that view.'

Hugh nodded. 'Have you been painting all morning?'

'Good heavens, no – I've been dashing around doing masses of chores.'

'I didn't hear you.'

'Well, I'm not exactly an elephant, am I?'

Hugh looked down at her. Her eyes were mischievous, her face was tilted. On an impulse, he bent and kissed her. 'No,' he said, 'I guess you aren't.'

In the afternoon, with a useful couple of thousand words behind him, Hugh took another walk.

This time he turned to the left, towards the sluice and the head of Smallgains and the boats. The day was again fine and warm. He sauntered along, his jacket hooked over his shoulder, enjoying the sun and the view and not bothering for the moment about his story. He was thinking about

Debbie, and how pleasant it was to have her around. It wasn't just that she was attractive – though that one kiss had somehow made him more aware of her attraction. They also got along so well – which was quite something, considering how suddenly and intimately they'd been thrown together. A week ago, he wouldn't have believed he could have lived happily at such close quarters with any woman. Of course, their tastes were similar. And their outlook. Debbie enjoyed contrast in her life – that was obvious. So did he. A bit of country and a bit of town. Peace and quiet – but not all the time ... She was stimulating, too. At least, she stimulated him ... And independent. Getting on with her own pursuits. Not fussing him. Quite a paragon. He'd never known a woman like her – and he'd known a few ...

He paused at the head of Smallgains, gazing around. The tide was flowing fast and the rills were filling. There were a lot more people about today, mostly picnic parties. Several groups were basking at the foot of the wall, children were swimming, a youth was paddling around in a canoe. A sailing dinghy had turned in the narrow channel below the footbridge and was punching its way back against the tide in a shower of spray. Always there was something to look at ...

He strolled on. Presently he came to the point where the sea wall and the built-up road converged. As he'd guessed, there was an anchorage just beyond. There was also a boatyard and a jetty. The creek was much wider here than higher up, and it evidently had water in it at all states of the tide. Some quite large cabin yachts and cruisers were riding at permanent moorings, flanked in the shallows by scores of smaller craft. Out in the channel there was a lot of activity – sailing dinghies weaving about, people working on the decks of their boats, a man having trouble trying to control a round rubber raft with a single paddle, another wrestling with a recalcitrant outboard motor. Hugh stood watching an old boatman who was painting a hull with loving care.

'You've got the right day for that,' he said, as the man looked up.

'Ah – it's grand.'

'Quite a lively spot here, isn't it?'

The boatman glanced across the water. He had the furrowed face of a man who'd spent his life squinting against the sun. 'Yes, we get plenty of folk down here at weekends ... Not many in the week, though.'

'No?'

The man shook his head. 'You wouldn't know it ... Specially now the season's coming to an end. We'll be starting to lay up soon.'

He returned to his painting. Hugh sauntered to the end of the jetty and sat down with his legs over the edge, watching the scene, storing up impressions. The place was full of interest. It was the kind of place, he thought, that might come in useful some day as the background for a story ...

Debbie was sitting at the window, reading, when he got back. She looked up with a welcoming smile as he entered. 'Did you have a pleasant walk?' she asked.

'So pleasant that I wished you could be there,' Hugh said. 'You'd have liked it ...' He described the lively scene at the boatyard.

'Well, thank you for the thought, anyway.'

'It's ridiculous that you should be stuck indoors in this lovely weather. I feel a pig, going off and leaving you ...'

'I'm quite happy,' Debbie said. 'I am used to being on my own, you know.'

'All the same, it's so pointless ...'

There was a crackle from the intercom loudspeaker beside them and Trant's voice suddenly filled the room. 'Mr Freeman, would you come up here, please?' There was urgency in his tone.

Hugh made a face. 'I thought the Supremo intended to sleep in the afternoons ...!' He pressed the switch, said 'Coming,' and climbed to the loft. Trant was standing at the slit window facing the creek, looking out through an

108

enormous pair of binoculars. Norris was beside him.

'A man's been watching the house through glasses for nearly five minutes,' Trant said. 'He's on the sea wall, close to the viewpoint. Take a look – but keep your head down.'

Hugh bent to the binoculars and peered through them, adjusting the focus. The magnification was enormous – he could distinguish individual blades of grass on the wall. But that was all. 'I can't see anyone,' he said.

'He's lying on the landward side of the wall – right on the bend. If you look closely, you can just make out his head through the grass.'

Hugh moved the glasses slightly – and stopped. He could see a face now, clamped to another pair of binoculars. Intent, motionless... 'Yes, you're right,' he said. There was dismay in his voice. 'Of course, he could be just looking at the mill...'

'Well, let's check.' Trant spoke into the intercom again. 'Debbie, would you come up? Quick as you can, please.'

She was there within seconds. Hugh gave her the glasses and told her where to look. She found the spot, and held it.

The watcher suddenly raised his head. They could all see him now, without glasses. He looked carefully around – then got to his feet and walked rapidly away along the wall.

Debbie passed the binoculars back. 'I believe it's the man who collected the photograph,' she said. 'I'm almost sure it is.'

Norris and Trant exchanged glances.

'I guess we're in business,' Norris said.

THREE

Chapter One

HUGH LAY awake for hours that night, milling over the alarming turn of events, trying to adjust his mind to the stark realities of the new situation.

The sighting of the watcher had come as a tremendous shock to him – much more so than to Debbie. He'd been so sure that the gang wouldn't show up, so confident that nothing would happen. If he'd believed otherwise, he'd never have let Trant persuade him to come to the mill. He'd have done his best to stop Debbie coming – instead of encouraging her ... Well, he'd been wrong. Crassly, obstinately wrong. He'd been living in cloud cuckoo land, believing what he wanted to. Treating the police as idiots. He felt ashamed now of the role he'd played – of his cheap witticisms and facetious cracks. It had been the flippancy of ignorance.

He ought to have had more regard for Trant's experience. Trant was the expert, the man who knew the underworld ... Not that the superintendent had proved his point about the jewels. The gang had tried to kill Debbie before there was any question of the jewels being lost – merely to protect Clay. That could still be their motive. But Hugh didn't think so. With half a million pounds worth of booty cached away, would they have been prepared to take huge new risks – infinitely greater risks, now that Debbie was guarded – just to save a fellow member of the gang? Did honour among thieves go so far? It seemed more likely that Trant was also right about the jewels. That Clay *had* hidden them, and that the gang *hadn't* been able to find them ...

And if he'd been right about so much, he could well be right about the next move, too. He knew these gangster types – he knew what they were capable of, the lengths to which they'd go. An attack on the mill, which a few hours before had seemed to Hugh a preposterous notion, now appeared rather more than probable. Obviously *something* was going to happen – the gang weren't watching the house for nothing. And with Debbie firmly shut away, how else could they get at her except by an armed assault? At any moment, the buzzer might go again – and this time it would be the real thing . . . With Debbie as the target.

Hugh had begun by thinking Trant's plan ridiculous. Now it suddenly seemed outrageous.

In fact, the night passed quietly – but by morning Hugh had worked up a considerable head of steam, and at break-fast it came out with a rush.

'Look, Superintendent,' he said, 'now that Debbie's been seen by the gang, surely there's no need for her to go on staying here?'

Trant turned a cold eye on him. 'Indeed there is, Mr Freeman.'

'Why . . .? Hasn't she done the job she came for?'

'Only partly,' Trant said. 'We know the gang's had the house under observation, but we don't know that they're entirely satisfied yet about Debbie . . . In any case, they're bound to have it in mind that she may be moved around for safety – and they'll be checking up every day to make sure she's still here. Unless they're sure, they won't attack.'

'So you intend to keep her here as live bait until the attack comes?'

'I'm afraid I must,' Trant said. 'That was always the idea.'

'Well, I don't think it's fair to Debbie . . . If you can't carry on without her, I think you ought to call the whole thing off.'

'Call it off . . .!' Trant looked at him in astonishment. 'At this stage?'

'Yes,' Hugh said. 'It's all much too dangerous.'

'It's no more dangerous than it was when Debbie agreed

to co-operate – and when *you* did. I put the position squarely to both of you.'

'That's true,' Hugh said. 'But at the time I didn't take you seriously ... It's clear now that you were right and I was wrong. Stupidly wrong. I admit it ... But the fact remains that when I came here I didn't believe anything would happen. Now I do. So for me, the position's changed.'

Trant looked at Debbie. 'What about you ...? *You* believed something would happen, didn't you?'

'I suppose so,' Debbie said, with a troubled glance at Hugh. 'You told us it would.'

'Exactly ... I told you that things would get very unpleasant, and that when they did it would be too late for you to change your mind ... I also told you that there'd be no danger for you personally – and I still say so. I believe we've got the situation well under control.'

'You believe,' Hugh said, 'but you don't *know* ... Everyone makes a mistake once in a while – even a Supremo ... You said yourself you expected the gang to come with machine guns – so you'll have no advantage there. Suppose they turn out to be quicker on the trigger than you and Norris? Suppose they blaze away directly the door's open? Suppose they shoot the spotlight out so that you can't see them? Battles don't always go according to plan.'

'You're an expert on battles, Mr Freeman?'

'I know there've been plenty of commanders who thought they were going to win and didn't ... You've no right to risk Debbie's life on a hope.'

'I insist I'm not doing,' Trant said. 'Every advantage will be with us. We shall be expecting them – we shall be ready. They won't be. All they'll be expecting is one lightly armed guard. And Norris and I have been specially trained in the use of our weapons. I'm quite confident of the result ... However, it's up to Debbie. She knows the position. Obviously I can't keep her here against her will ... It's for her to decide.'

Hugh said, 'Debbie, I think you should leave. I'll take you in the car, and we'll find somewhere else for you to hide.

Almost any place would be safer than this one now. The police will give you protection wherever you are – they'll have to if they want you as a witness. Isn't that right, Superintendent?'

'Of course,' Trant said.

'So you'll have nothing to lose and everything to gain... Honestly, Debbie, I don't think you realize what you may be in for if you stay here.'

'I know there may be a fight,' Debbie said.

'Yes, but it's just a word to you... You can paint a picture – but can you *imagine* one? Try and think – now, while it's not too late ... The bloody mess, the agony, the hellish din ... The wrong chaps getting shot ... Some thug breaking into your room and pouring bullets into you... It could happen... Superintendent, can you look Debbie in the eye and swear there's absolutely no chance that things might go wrong? No chance whatever...?'

For a moment, Trant hesitated. Then he said, 'Well, there's always the outside chance. The thousand-to-one chance. I'm not denying that... It's all a question of what's a reasonable risk. We've an excellent prospect now of putting paid to this gang for good – and that's surely worth a slight risk?'

'It is for you,' Hugh said. 'It isn't for Debbie...'

'Have you the right to speak for her?'

'Yes, I have,' Hugh said furiously. 'Who's going to protect her from you if I don't? You're as ruthless and calculating as the gang you're trying to catch. You're using your position and authority to keep a young and inexperienced girl in obvious danger for your own professional ends. I think it's monstrous... No doubt you'd consider it a very satisfactory exchange if you got the whole gang, and Debbie was shot.'

'That's quite untrue,' Trant said, 'and I deeply resent your saying it ... I've told you again and again that in my view there's virtually no danger for Debbie. If I'd thought there'd be any appreciable danger, I wouldn't have let her come. I'd have relied on the stand-in... Now she is here, the whole enterprise depends on her. If she leaves, all our efforts will have been wasted and the gang will go free.'

'In the circumstances,' Hugh said, 'I'd be prepared to let them.'

Trant gave a faint sigh. 'Well, you've a right to your own set of values, Mr Freeman – your own standards of civic responsibility... If you think it proper to stay on the sidelines where crime's concerned, you're entitled to your view – and God knows you'll find plenty of company there. The sidelines are a very comfortable place – sometimes I wouldn't mind being there myself... I'll just say this. If these men we're after go free, within months they'll be robbing again – and probably killing again. And they'll go on robbing and killing until someone has the guts to stop them...'

Debbie looked uncertainly at Hugh.

Hugh said, 'Can Debbie and I talk alone, Superintendent?'

'Of course,' Trant said. 'Sergeant, let's go upstairs...'

Hugh was the first to break the silence. 'I suppose I hadn't any right to speak for you... But I can't bear to think something might happen to you.'

'I know...'

'Trant's using you, Debbie. He's using me, too. He ought to have been a puppetmaster... He's going to have his showdown whatever it costs. And it's bound to be frightful... Surely you don't want to stay?'

'Of course I don't want to,' Debbie said. 'I'm beginning to feel horribly scared... But...'

'But what?'

'It isn't an easy decision, is it...? Are we even sure it would be safe for me to leave?'

'Why shouldn't it be?'

'Suppose the gang were watching? Wouldn't they try to do something when they saw me going?'

'You mean like ambushing the car along the private road?'

'Something like that ... It wouldn't be difficult at night, would it?'

'Well, we could go in the daytime,' Hugh said. 'To-morrow morning ... We'd take a good look round first and make sure there was no one lurking about – then we'd be quite safe. And Trant would give us an armed escort. The gang wouldn't have a chance.'

'Perhaps not ...' Debbie looked very troubled. 'Of course, I did promise him that I'd stay. I said I'd see it through to the end. Quite voluntarily. I knew I was going to be used. And he did rely on me ... So I would be letting him down if I went.'

'For heaven's sake, Debbie, this isn't the time for school-girl loyalty ... Your life's in danger.'

'He doesn't think it is ... And he has been right so far. I've quite a lot of faith in him.'

Hugh stared at her, his expression a mixture of curiosity and exasperation. 'I don't understand you ... First you say it wouldn't be safe to go. Then you say it would be letting Trant down. Now you say you've faith in him ... What's really in your mind?'

There was a little silence. Then Debbie said, 'I suppose it's what he said about standing on the sidelines ... I'm wondering how I'll feel if I do go.'

'What do you mean?'

'I'm sure he was right about those men. They will go on killing.'

'I expect they will,' Hugh said. 'If they don't other men will. Crime never stops. That's why we've got police ... It's not your affair. It's only by chance that you happen to be involved at all.'

'I know ... But I *am* involved – nothing can alter that. It does depend on me whether these particular men go on killing or not ... If I leave now, I'll be running away from a responsibility because it's going to be unpleasant.'

'I don't see it that way,' Hugh said. 'It's a responsibility that ought never to have been placed on you – so you've a right to run ... I'm certainly prepared to run with you.'

'It's different for you,' Debbie said. 'You're only thinking about me – you just want me to be safe... If you took me out of here, you'd feel you'd achieved something – you'd still be able to look yourself in the face... But I wouldn't. Every time I read about a night watchman being coshed, I'd wonder if it was my fault. I'd always feel ashamed of what I'd done... No one wants to get into danger – but once you're in it, surely you've got to see it through...' Tears sprang to her eyes. 'I don't want to spend the rest of my life despising myself. I'd sooner be dead.'

Hugh looked at her for a little while without speaking. Then he gave a resigned shrug. 'All right, Debbie... I've said my piece – I won't argue any more.'

'You're not angry with me?'

'Of course not.'

'Will you tell Trant?'

'If you like,' Hugh said.

The superintendent was stretched out on his bed, talking to Norris. He raised himself on an elbow as Hugh entered. 'Yes, Mr Freeman?'

'Debbie's decided to stay. I couldn't talk her out of it.'

'I didn't suppose you would,' Trant said.

'I still think she'll regret it.'

'We shall see... Perhaps *you'd* like to leave, Mr Freeman...? It would be awkward – but I dare say we could manage without you now.'

'Don't be bloody silly,' Hugh said.

Chapter Two

OUTWARDLY, the situation at the mill that day hardly differed from the preceding days. Having already made his dispositions to meet all foreseeable contingencies, Trant saw no need to change anything merely because the threat had moved nearer. He and Norris continued to do their shifts in the loft, resting and scanning the saltings by turns. Hugh went into the village to buy tobacco and the Sunday newspapers. Debbie prepared the meals and dutifully showed herself at the window from time to time throughout the day. Leigh kept up his patrol in the warm sun. The superficial serenity of the mill was undisturbed by anything harsher than the voices and laughter of visitors picnicking and playing radios and mudlarking by the sea wall and the rills. Everything seemed exactly the same as before.

Beneath the surface, nothing was the same. Security for the day might be guaranteed by the near presence of so many trippers – but the night would soon return. There was an atmosphere of tension, now, that in different ways affected everyone. Trant showed it by a studied calm – the commander setting an example to his men. Norris showed it by cleaning his already spotless gun. Leigh was more alert and suspicious on watch. He kept a particularly sharp eye on a no-longer-youthful couple who'd arrived on a motor bike and pitched a tent in the field just beyond the conifers. He couldn't see why they should have come so near the house when there were miles of empty sea wall available – and he didn't much care for the look of the man. He reported their activities to Trant and continued to watch them from a distance. But there was nothing in their behaviour to suggest that they had designs on the house. Presently they disappeared into the tent and closed the flap. Their designs were evidently on each other ...

Debbie spent a miserable day. She couldn't help thinking, as the afternoon wore on, that Hugh might have been right after all and that perhaps she had been quixotic in her decision to stay. It was one thing to take a high-minded stand on a bright morning and another to face the approaching consequences as the day drew to a close. It worried her that she'd virtually forced Hugh to stay, too. Trant had guaranteed *her* safety – but not Hugh's. And it worried her that, temporarily at least, she felt estranged from him. The carefree relationship of the early days had gone and constraint had taken its place. They seemed separated by the gulf of their disagreement.

Hugh was moody and irritable, nursing his resentment of Trant, deeply apprehensive about what was going to happen, and quite unable to work. Concentration was a tender plant that couldn't survive the least disturbance – let alone the early prospect of attempted murder. He walked without pleasure along the sea wall, glowering at everyone he met, seeing a possible member of the gang in every unaccompanied male. The faceless killers were only too real to him now. He wondered where their base was, and what time of night they'd come, and which night they'd choose . . . Now that they'd found Debbie's hide-out, it must be soon. They wouldn't want to risk her being moved. Probably they'd come that night. He almost hoped they would. Waiting for the blow to fall, living it in imagination, was almost worse than meeting it. Better to get it over . . .

There was an unexpected alarm in the late afternoon, setting everyone's nerves tingling and testing Trant's daytime organization. Norris, from the loft, suddenly announced on the intercom, 'Large black car approaching from the village along the private road.' A moment later the front door slammed shut as Leigh rushed in to make a similar announcement and grab his gun. Trant, dishevelled from his bed but fully alert, joined him in the entrance hall with his own gun. Hugh went to the head of the stairs. Debbie stood tensely by the sitting-room door.

The noise of the approaching car grew suddenly louder as Trant switched on the outside microphones. It was turning into the forecourt. It had stopped . . . Then, disconcertingly, a chuckle came through the intercom. 'It's okay,' Norris said softly. 'There are kids in it.'

Hugh went down to the hall. Through the door, he heard a young voice shrill, 'It's a dead end, Dad.' A woman's voice said, 'Funny looking place, isn't it?' There was a scraping of gears, the engine revved up, and the car departed.

Trant switched off the mikes. 'Pity some people can't read,' he said. 'There goes my beauty sleep!'

Tension mounted again as dusk approached. The two night men ate their dinner quickly, and in silence. Leigh made a final check outside the building, noting that the camping couple had packed up their tent and were making leisurely preparations to depart. Trant and Norris took up their stations in the hall. Leigh did his curtain round, and joined Hugh and Debbie for dinner. Afterwards, the three of them sat reading the Sunday papers in the sitting-room. Outside, all was quiet.

It stayed that way till shortly after dark. Then, around nine o'clock, the intercom crackled again and Trant spoke. 'What's burning?' he asked.

Hugh flicked down the switch. 'Nothing up here,' he said.

'There's a fire somewhere – I can smell it. Have a look round, will you?'

'Yes – all right.'

Debbie was already on her way to the kitchen. There was nothing wrong there. Hugh looked in the bedrooms. Together they climbed to the loft. Hugh sniffed. There *was* a smell of fire. But everything seemed in order in the room. They went to the windows.

'There it is!' Debbie exclaimed. Hugh joined her and looked down. There was smoke and a flicker of flame in the dry, hay-strewn grass beyond the conifers. Hugh reported on the intercom. 'Those campers must have dropped a cigarette end,' he said.

'Is it spreading?' Trant's voice was sharp.

'I think it is ... The wind's blowing this way ...' As Hugh spoke, the flames leapt higher. Suddenly, with an explosive crackle, the haystack caught. 'Yes – it's getting worse. Much worse ... I think it's going to spread to the trees.'

'I'm coming up,' Trant said. 'Leigh, bring your gun and take over down here.'

In a matter of seconds the superintendent was beside

them at the window, staring down. Some of the dead trees at the edge of the copse had already caught. Flames and sparks were shooting twenty feet into the air.

'If it reaches the house, the whole place will go up,' Trant muttered. 'Those weather boards will burn like tinder.' He stood eyeing the blaze. For once, he seemed uncertain what to do.

'Is there time to get an engine out?' Hugh said.

'Not a hope...' The flames gave another leap – and Trant's hesitancy passed. 'We'll have to tackle it ourselves... Come on.'

Momentarily, Hugh blocked the way. 'I've just had a thought,' he said. 'Suppose it wasn't a cigarette end? Suppose it's the gang – trying to smoke us out...? They could be waiting for us.'

'I know that,' Trant said impatiently.

'Then isn't this the time to call up your reinforcements, Superintendent?'

'No...!' Trant brushed past him. 'We'd be roasted by the time they got here... We'll have to take a chance.' He went quickly down the stairs. At the sitting-room landing he turned. 'Stay here as long as you can, Debbie... If the place gets too hot for you, go down and stand behind the front door.'

Debbie nodded. Her face was pale. 'Be careful,' she called to Hugh, as he passed her. He gave her hand a quick squeeze, and followed the superintendent down.

In the entrance hall, Trant spoke briefly to his troops above the mounting uproar of the fire. 'We'll have to risk it,' he said. 'We've no choice ... This could be the showdown – so keep your eyes skinned.'

He opened the door cautiously and peered out. The front of the house, and a wide area around it, was brilliantly lit by the red flames. Beyond, there were shadows. Dangerous, concealing shadows... He stepped out, eyes narrowed, gun swivelling, his finger tight on the trigger. This was the moment...

Nothing happened.

'Seems all right,' he called. 'Leigh, you stay by the door ... Norris, keep us covered ... If anyone shoots, blaze away ... Come on, Freeman.'

Hugh raced with him across the exposed forecourt. The need for action kept his mind off bullets. By now the whole corpse was an inferno. The boards at the corner of the house had caught and were burning furiously. It was going to be touch and go. Hugh dragged the hose from the garage and joined it to the tap. The pressure was poor – the water came out in a sagging loop rather than a jet. But the loop was high enough to reach the burning boards. Trant took the hose and played the water on the corner of the house, quenching the flames, soaking the charred wood around them. Hugh did what he could with a bucket and water from a rain tank, hurling gallon after gallon into the trees. The heat was intense, the noise deafening, the smoke blinding.

There was no question of mastering the flames – only of keeping them away from the house. And that, little by little, they achieved. In fifteen minutes they'd cleared a sufficient area to make sure that the mill was safe. In twenty, the consuming fire in the heart of the conifers had reached its peak. In half an hour, all that was left of the copse was collapsing in a soggy, smouldering heap.

'Right – let's get in,' Trant said. Sweating and panting, they made for the entrance hall. Norris backed in after them. Leigh followed them, and closed the door.

They were barely inside when the telephone rang. Trant moved towards it – then remembered, and motioned to Leigh. Leigh said, 'Tide Mill here ... Yes, we're okay, thanks ... No, it was only some trees outside ... Not at all – very kind of you to ring ... 'Bye.' He hung up. 'Someone in the village who saw the flames,' he said.

Trant nodded.

Debbie was standing at the top of the stairs. 'All right?' she called down anxiously.

'Yes, it's out,' Hugh said. 'No casualties...! How about you?'

'I'm fine... The plaster's all cracked in the sitting-room – it's in a terrible mess.'

'So are we,' Hugh said.

'Would you like me to bring some beer down? I'm sure I'll be quite safe – just for a minute.'

'Very well,' Trant said. 'We can certainly do with it...' He looked at Hugh. 'Nice work, Mr Freeman... You did a good job.'

Hugh brushed a smouldering twig from his trousers. 'Even a non-combatant can fight a fire,' he said.

Trant grunted. 'A bad slip-up on my part... Fire was something I never thought of.'

Hugh gazed at him in mock astonishment. 'You mean – even Homer nods!'

'I'm afraid so. I should have had those trees down. It was a serious oversight...'

'Could I have that in writing, Superintendent?'

Trant permitted himself a thin smile.

Norris said, 'So it *was* an accidental fire, sir, after all.'

'Yes,' Trant said. 'We were lucky.'

Hugh was helping Debbie to clear up the mess in the sitting-room. Leigh had gone to the loft to keep an eye on the smouldering debris outside. The night men were back at their posts.

Hugh said, 'Of course, Trant *should* have called up his reinforcements. They might have been too late for the fire – but they could have made all the difference in a battle. He took a big risk.'

'It would have been the end of his plan,' Debbie said. 'He'd never have been able to keep the hide-out a secret if a lot of cars had come roaring through the village.'

'Exactly... It's just as I said – he puts the plan above everything. Even you. If we'd all been shot down, they'd obviously have got you, too.'

Debbie poured a dustpan-full of plaster into a pail. 'Well, it didn't happen.'

'Not this time ... Mind you, one has to hand it to him – he behaved magnificently. The way he stepped out of that door into the open was really something to watch.'

'He seemed to think you were pretty good, too ... Perhaps you and he will bury the hatchet now.'

'Maybe,' Hugh said. 'But I guess we'll both mark the spot!'

To Hugh's surprise, the night again passed quietly. After his exertions he even slept quite well. It was while he was shaving next morning – always a time for vigorous mental activity – that he began to wonder again about the fire.

They'd all taken it for granted that it had been an accident, because nothing had happened – but, now that he thought about it, it was hard to see how those campers could have started it. According to Leigh, they'd been packing up to leave around eight o'clock – and it had been after nine when he and Debbie had spotted the fire. It had been quite a small fire, too, when they'd first seen it. If the campers had dropped a cigarette or a match before they left, the blaze would surely have been much bigger by nine. That dry grass wouldn't just have quietly smouldered away in the same spot for an hour ... At least, Hugh didn't think so.

He dressed and put on his gumboots and went out to have a look round. Wisps of smoke were still curling up from the heart of the burned-out copse. He skirted the edge of it and came out in the field where the tent had been. The site was clearly marked by a rectangle of beaten grass. The nearest bit of the fire-blackened area, he saw, was twenty yards from it ... Of course, one of the campers could easily have strolled that far and flung a cigarette end down. All the same ...

Hugh walked slowly round the edge of the burned grass, glancing up at the loft window from time to time to check his position. This must have been about the place where the fire started ... Suddenly he stopped. There were some bits of paper in the ashes. Bits of newspaper, screwed up into spills – charred, but not completely consumed. He picked one of them up. There was an odd smell about it. He put it to his nose, and sniffed. Paraffin ...!

So the fire hadn't been an accident after all – it had been started deliberately. And not by the campers – they'd been too long gone. In any case, why would they have wanted to start a fire ...? It was much more likely that the gang had done it. And that meant, surely, that they *had* been around while the fire was being put out. They would hardly have started it and gone away. It would have been a pointless thing to do ...

Hugh stood cogitating for a while. Then he went back into the house to tell Trant what he'd found.

Norris said, 'If they were around, why didn't they attack? We were sitting ducks – they couldn't have hoped for a better opportunity.'

He and Trant were having breakfast. Hugh and Debbie were with them. Leigh was on watch in the loft.

'There could have been several reasons,' Hugh said. 'They may not have been armed. Or not adequately armed. After all, you'd got a formidable lot of weapons between you ... Or perhaps there was only one of them ... *I* think it was a reconnaissance.'

Trant looked at him sharply. 'To check on the strength of the guard, you mean?'

'It would have been a sensible thing to do, wouldn't it, before they took any action? They'd seen Leigh – they might have wanted to make sure that he really was the only one ... And what better way than to smoke us out with an apparently accidental fire, and see who emerged ...? I can't think of anything else that covers the situation.'

There was a little silence. Then Norris said, 'Well, if they *were* still around, and they saw three men armed with automatic rifles, I'd say the trap's sprung, and we've had it.'

'You think they won't attack?' Hugh said hopefully.

'I can't see them wanting to face that armament – even for a half a million ... What do you say, sir?'

'I don't know,' Trant said. 'It's a lot of money – they're not going to abandon it lightly ... And as far as they know, they can still take us unawares. They're probably rather surprised that we're here in such strength – but they've no reason to believe we're actually lying in wait for them.'

'Wouldn't they think it a bit suspicious, sir, that two of the well-armed guards they saw hadn't shown themselves outside the building until they were absolutely forced to?'

'They might wonder about it, Sergeant – but it's a long way from that to suspecting a trap, when there's no other reason to do so. I doubt if it's even occurred to them. And if it hasn't, they'll probably still think they can catch us off balance and shoot us up before we're ready.'

Norris looked dubious. 'I reckon they'd need a howitzer, sir, to make the risk worth while.'

'Or a new idea,' Hugh said.

Trant regarded him thoughtfully. 'Still harping on that, Mr Freeman?'

'Well, they've shown it's possible ... The fire was new.'

'True ... Have you any fresh suggestions?'

'I'm afraid not.'

'H'm ...' Trant sat quietly for a while, considering the position. Then he pushed his plate back and got up. 'Well,' he said, 'the fact is we don't know what they'll do now ... We'll just have to wait and see.'

Chapter Three

THERE WAS a disturbing change in the weather that afternoon. Around two o'clock, a heavy sea mist came rolling up the estuary, forcing Trant to institute something like his night dispositions in the daytime. With visibility reduced to a few yards, neither Leigh on patrol nor the loft look-out could give any useful warning of the approach of danger. The gang could creep up on the house as easily now as after dark. Trant therefore brought Leigh into the entrance hall, and for the rest of the day two men were constantly on duty in the watch chairs with guns at the ready and the mikes switched on. It was an edgy day for everyone. Until now, the daylight hours at least had offered some respite from anxiety. With a blanket of mist shrouding the mill, there could be no relaxation at all. A cold draught blowing through the house added to the general discomfort. It was a relief when darkness fell and the familiar routines could be resumed in the lighted rooms behind drawn curtains.

As he sat in his guard chair that night, Trant's thoughts reverted to the fire and its possible consequences. In the light of the evidence, he'd very little doubt that the gang *had* been watching the garrison – and though he'd said the defenders would have to 'wait and see' what happened next, he wasn't the man to wait passively. The situation had changed – and his defences must be reviewed.

One thing was clear. If the gang attacked expecting to meet three well-armed men instead of one lightly-armed one, there were obviously going to be increased risks for the garrison. The gang would be more wary in its approach, more alert. They'd be keyed up for a stiff fight. They'd be all set to get their shots in first. To that extent, the odds had undoubtedly changed in their favour.

However, there'd still be surprises in store for them. They would hardly be expecting to find a reception committee waiting for them in the entrance hall. Even if they were, the spotlight would still blind them. No doubt they'd try to shoot the light out, as Freeman had said. No doubt they would blaze away in all directions. But with a visible target to aim at from the first moment, the defenders would have an enormous advantage. The risks still seemed to Trant acceptable – considering what was at stake. Especially if he took the extra precautions that were already in his mind . . .

He turned to the other possibility – the one that Freeman had kept bringing up. That the gang would try to think of some alternative to a direct assault. Trant's mind was by no means closed to the danger. Certainly less closed than it had been. Systematically he went over all his defence arrangements from the beginning, trying to spot some weakness, some loophole that he'd overlooked. Had he an Achilles' heel? He could think of nothing. As long as the electric strips and the mikes continued to function – and why shouldn't they? – surprise was impossible. Any approach would be signalled. *Any* approach . . . So what unforeseen danger could there be? It would need more than ingenuity to put Debbie in jeopardy from a distance. There were limits, after all, to the facilities the gang could command. They could hardly get hold of a tank, or a helicopter, or a piece of artillery. An attack with automatic weapons still seemed their best bet. And against such an attack, the mill was adequately safeguarded. Trant's rethinking had brought him full circle.

A blustery forty-eight hours followed the mist. Strong winds howled around the mill and moaned like banshees in the microphones at night. By day, the sea wall and the saltings were empty of all but the most hardy visitors. The only holiday-makers Hugh saw while the spell of bad weather lasted were a small, bedraggled group cowering from the westerly wind in one of the few sheltered spots – the bend at the head of Smallgains Rill. The look-out from the loft reported an occasional pedestrian on the wall in the far distance, but no more activity at the viewpoint. Trant was quick to point out that that didn't mean the watching was over. Now that Debbie's identity had presumably been established, her continued presence at the mill could easily be checked from much further away. Any one of those pedestrians might be a scout for the gang.

The other members of the garrison shared a growing scepticism about the prospects as the day went by. Hugh swung between fears of the unexpected, and hope that the gang had gone for good – with hope tipping the scale. Debbie, growing restive at being shut up all the time when nothing was happening, tried without success to persuade Trant to let her take an occasional constitutional. Norris was still sticking to his view that there'd be no direct attack and that the gang had probably left. Leigh seemed to be of the same opinion. Since the night of the fire, he'd taken to going for a short stroll immediately after dinner each evening, announcing his return by a word in the microphone. Invariably he reported a total lack of activity on the sea wall and the saltings.

Trant, alone, was unimpressed by what he called the 'lull'. He rejected out of hand a renewed suggestion from Hugh that the enterprise should be called off. He restated his belief that an attack would come soon. With Clay's committal proceedings less than a week away, he said, the gang must be in a state of desperation. It was just a question of holding on ... Far from relaxing his measures, he strengthened them. To meet the possibility that the intruders might open fire directly the door swung back, he set up new defences. Hugh was dispatched to Colchester to buy sacks which Leigh laboriously filled at dusk with dried mud from the edge of the saltings. Before long, there were substantial earthworks round the two chairs in the entrance hall ...

It wasn't until the evening of the twelfth day at the mill that any new break came in the quiet and ordered life of the garrison.

Hugh and Debbie had just finished washing up after dinner and were chatting in a relaxed way in the sitting-room. Leigh was out on his usual walk. Trant and Norris were on watch below. Suddenly the intercom came alive. 'Would you come down here, Mr Freeman?' Trant said.

Hugh went down. He found Trant standing by his sand-bagged chair, looking vaguely worried. 'What is it, Superintendent?'

'Leigh's a long time out tonight,' Trant said.

Hugh glanced at his watch. It was half past nine. 'Yes, he is – he's been gone more than an hour.'

'He's only supposed to stay out half an hour,' Trant said. 'He had clear instructions to that effect.'

'Did he say where he was going?'

'No, but he always goes along the wall – one way or the other. Sometimes to the boatyard, sometimes past the view-point . . . He could have had a fall – sprained an ankle . . .'

'Didn't he take a torch?'

'Yes, a good one – that big metal one . . . But it's a rough walk, even with a light.'

Hugh nodded. 'Would you like me to go and look for him?'

'I would, if you don't mind . . . You're the only one who can.'

'Okay – I'll be down in a second . . .' Hugh went up to his room, put on his gumboots, and collected the big handlamp he'd brought from the cottage. On the way down he looked in on Debbie. 'Leigh's playing truant,' he said. 'Trant wants me to fetch him in. I shan't be long . . .'

The night was heavily overcast and threatening rain, but somewhere behind the clouds there was a nearly full moon and the darkness was far from absolute. Across the saltings, the flowing tide gleamed silver in the channel. Hugh stood on top of the wall, gazing around. If Leigh was walking on the wall, his torch should be visible. But there was no sign of any light. If he'd fallen, of course, the torch could be hidden in the grass . . . Hugh set off at a brisk pace in the direction of the boatyard, swinging the handlamp beam so that it illuminated both slopes of the wall in turn, planting his gumboots firmly on the uneven, slippery surface as he walked. He reached the yard in a little over ten minutes and stood there, looking about him and listening. Except for the untenanted yachts swinging at their moorings in the anchorage, there was little sound and no movement. Ahead, the sea wall stretched away for empty miles. Hugh felt sure Leigh wouldn't have gone on there. He'd have known he'd be back late, and he wasn't a man to disregard orders. Obviously he hadn't come this way at all. Hugh retraced his steps.

He stopped at the mill and announced himself into the microphone. Trant opened the door. 'Is he back?' Hugh asked.

'No,' Trant said.

'Well, there's no sign of him between here and the boat-yard... I'll have to look the other way...' Hugh paused, suddenly uneasy. 'You don't think he could have run into – trouble – do you?'

'With the gang, you mean?' Trant shook his head. 'I shouldn't think so. I had a good look round just before dusk, and there wasn't a soul in sight. In the normal way he'd have been back before anyone could get here – that's why I let him go when he did. It was the safe time... Anyway, I wouldn't expect them to show up till much later in the night.'

'I suppose not,' Hugh said. 'All right, I'll try the other way...' He set off towards the viewpoint.

Debbie pressed the intercom switch and spoke into the receiver. 'Are you there, Superintendent?'

There was a click. 'Yes, Debbie.'

'I thought I heard voices... What's going on?'

'Mr Freeman's still looking for Leigh. He's gone the other way, now.'

'What do you suppose has happened?'

'I should think Leigh has had some sort of fall,' Trant said. 'Probably slipped down the wall... Don't worry, Debbie, I'm sure we'll hear something quite soon.'

'I'll be glad when they're back.'

'We all will,' Trant said.

Hugh reached the viewpoint without seeing any sign of the sergeant. He continued on along the wall, still flashing his lamp down both slopes. He walked for fifteen minutes by his watch and then paused again, as he'd done at the boatyard. This should have been Leigh's limit. He directed the lamp beam in a circle around him, signalling his presence. Several times he called Leigh's name. But there was no answering light, no cry from the darkness, no sound at all. He waited a few minutes, reluctant to give up. He was beginning to feel really worried now. What on earth could have happened to the fellow ...?

As he gazed out across the saltings, he suddenly had a most unpleasant thought. Could Leigh possibly have ventured into that wilderness of channels and rills and got caught in the mud? Surely he wouldn't have been so daft? Not in the dark. And with a rising tide ... Leigh was a level-headed chap. Yet all the more obvious possibilities seemed to be exhausted. Hugh turned and set off slowly back towards the mill, directing his light now down the seaward side of the wall, looking for any sign of a descent. As he approached the viewpoint for the second time, his swinging lamp drew a reflection from something on the marsh. A bright object, lying beside the footbridge path. He dropped down the wall and went up to it ... It was a large metal torch, switched off. *Leigh's torch* ...

He shone the handlamp around. There were footprints in the soft surface of the saltings – recent footprints, by the look of them. One set from the wall to the torch, then a whole mass of them around the torch, then several two-way tracks between the torch and a nearby rill. Hugh followed them. They ended in a great patch of churned-up mud on the bank of the rill. He shone his light down – and froze.

Sergeant Leigh was lying face upwards in the bottom of the rill. He was dead. One side of his skull had been crushed flat by some tremendous blow.

HUGH STAGGERED back to the sea wall and slumped to the ground. His head was whirling. He was going to be sick. He was going to faint. He thrust his head down between his knees, forcing back the fugitive blood . . . Slowly the nausea passed, leaving him soaked in sweat and shivering.

Fear and horror pinned him down. Leigh had been murdered by the gang. They might still be around. If they'd killed Leigh, they were just as likely to kill him. He was equally exposed and defenceless . . .

Then he took a grip on himself. He was no safer sitting than moving. He must try to get back and warn Trant. Tell him that an attack on the mill was imminent. It *must* be. That was why the gang had killed Leigh. They'd seen the triple guard on the night of the fire and they'd killed him to improve the odds before they struck. Now they'd attack at once. They'd have to. By killing him, they'd disclosed their presence. For them, it was now or never . . . Hugh struggled to his feet and set off back along the edge of the saltings, hugging the wall for protection, not using his lamp.

He stumbled on for fifty yards. Then he suddenly stopped short.

There was something here that he didn't understand. It was two hours since Leigh had left the mill. He must have been killed at least an hour and a half ago. Why hadn't the gang attacked right away? Why had they given time for Leigh's absence to be noted, for a search to start, for the garrison to become suspicious – and maybe call in reinforcements . . .? Already they'd missed the best, the only opportunity they could expect to have of achieving surprise. Could it be that they *didn't* intend to attack . . .?

In that case, why had they killed Leigh? Not, Hugh was sure, out of mere bloody-mindedness. They'd never have risked wrecking all their hopes for the pleasure of killing a policeman. They must have had some vital reason. Some reason that had *forced* them to kill a man strolling quietly along the sea wall in the dark . . .

Wait a minute! Leigh had descended the wall. On his own – voluntarily. From the wall to the place where the torch had been dropped, there'd been only one set of prints . . . Perhaps he'd heard something. The gang talking . . . Perhaps he'd gone to investigate. With his torch switched off. And they'd attacked him, there where the torch had fallen . . . But again, why? They could easily have melted away into the darkness when they'd heard him approaching. They'd have been in no danger from him. They hadn't *had* to give themselves away . . .

Unless they'd been up to something. Something they couldn't hide. That might be the answer. Some new plan . . . The plan that Hugh had always feared they'd think up . . . Leigh had stumbled on some secret activity – and they'd had to silence him . . . But what could they have been doing in this empty waste of mud and water . . .? They'd had some tool with them, by the look of Leigh's head. Some flat tool like a spade. What devilry were they plotting? What was going to happen? Whatever it was, it was going to happen quickly. Before daylight. Otherwise they'd surely have done something about Leigh's body. They could easily have buried it . . .

Hugh stood listening. Except for the rustle of the wind in the grass and the cry of a distant curlew, there wasn't a sound. No voices, no movement, no lights – nothing. For the moment, at any rate, the gang had gone. He turned and made his way back to the footpath, picking up the prints again. They stretched beyond the point where Leigh's body lay. He followed them, shining his lamp ahead. They led to the main channel. On the channel bank there was another churned-up patch of mud. He directed his lamp beam down the smooth, sloping side. At the bottom, the young tide was flowing. There were a lot of marks in the mud, rising from the water's edge. Two rows of deep holes made by booted feet – and between them, a straight, scored line. A boat had been dragged up here since the last tide. A rowing boat . . . There was a thin, rectangular hole near the bank that looked as though it had been made by the tip of an oar. Probably the gang had come by boat – rowing up at dusk on the first of the flood. That would explain how they'd appeared on the scene so quickly. If they'd come from the anchorage it would have taken them only a few minutes...

More prints led off in the direction of the footbridge. Hugh continued beside them. The planks of the bridge were wet and slippery with fresh mud. There'd been a lot of activity here. He started to cross. The structure felt more rickety than ever. In the centre, the planks sagged alarmingly. The whole thing seemed on the point of collapse. He leaned cautiously over the rail and flashed his lamp down...

He could hardly believe his eyes. Almost all the supports had gone. The piles had been sawn off where they joined the planks and the stumps dug out of the channel bed. The few that were left were widely spaced. The footbridge no longer obstructed the channel...

For a moment, Hugh stared down blankly. Then he crossed to the other side of the bridge and stood uncertainly on the bank. This, obviously, was what had attracted Leigh's attention. This was what he'd have seen and reported if he'd lived. This was why he'd been killed. But what did it mean? Presumably the bridge obstruction had been cleared to allow a boat to pass. Had the gang already gone up in their boat? It seemed unlikely. There was no sound from the mill, no indication of disturbance or alarm. And by now there would have been. Though the gang didn't know it, the microphones would have picked up the creak of oars in rowlocks long before the boat arrived. Or, if it had just drifted, the inevitable bump against the mill wheel. Boats were noisy things. Trant would have heard it – and he'd have taken some action... In any case, how would it have helped the gang to reach the mill by boat, when there was nothing to prevent them approaching it on foot from any direction...?

It was baffling. Hugh shone his torch around, seeking

some fresh clue to what had happened, to what might lie ahead. The beam picked out a heap of sawn-off piles and debris from the bridge, stacked on the bank, but nothing else. There were no footprints leading to the farther sea wall. If the gang hadn't gone on in their boat, it looked as though they'd rowed back the way they'd come...

He stood hesitating. He felt sure the answer to all the questions was here – yet there seemed no point in staying around in the dark. He'd better go and tell Trant what he'd found – and break the news about Leigh. He started back across the bridge, glancing up and down the creek. Suddenly he stopped. Fifty yards below the bridge, something was drifting on the silvery water. A patch of weed? A log? Or a boat...? It looked too solid for weed, too broad for a log... Hugh retreated to the bank and crouched down. The object drew nearer. Soon he was able to identify it by its shape. It was a round, inflated rubber dinghy – like the one he'd seen being manoeuvred in the anchorage a few days earlier. There was no one in it. The space encircled by the plump, inflated tube around it seemed to be covered over. The dinghy was black, silent – and sinister. Hugh suddenly knew that he'd got to stop it.

He moved quickly to the bank above the bridge and ploughed down the steep mud slope to the water's edge. The dinghy was just passing under the bridge. It touched one of the remaining supports, rotated a little, freed itself, and came on. It was five or six feet from the edge and moving fast. Hugh dragged a boot out of the sucking mud, took a step into the water, leaned forward, and lunged. His fingers closed on a loop and he drew the dinghy in.

He'd left his lamp up on the bank and he could see very little in the darkness – but he could feel. Over the whole well of the dinghy there was a convex roof of some tough, resilient material which met the inflated sides in a sealed joint. Under the bulge there was something large and solid. From inside came a slow, steady ticking.

The dinghy was a floating bomb!

Chapter Five

FOR A PARALYSING moment, Hugh felt incapable of
thought or action. He was aware only of the ticking clock –
and of the charge inside the bomb. At any second, it could
explode. At any second, he himself might disintegrate into
nothing...

Then reason returned. The bomb couldn't have been set
to go off yet – not for a few minutes, at least. The gang
would have had to allow time for it to reach the mill from
where it was now. He could count on those few minutes.
Time to do something. But what...?

Let the bomb go? Claw his way back up the slope, make
a dash for the mill, and get the garrison out? They could
take quick cover behind that bend in the wall, by the sluice.
It was the obvious thing to do. The thing he wanted to do –
desperately. It would be so easy – just to take his hand
away. Such a relief. But...

Suppose the bomb was timed to go off immediately it
reached the mill? It would float up there long before he
could get back himself, through the hazards of mud and
darkness, to raise the alarm. Trant would have no warning.
The rubber boat would make no sound, the ticking clock
wasn't loud enough to be heard through the mikes... Suppose the mill blew up before he got there – and Debbie was
killed...! It was an unthinkable gamble. There must be
another way...

Was there any chance of getting at the mechanism? – of
stopping the clock? Feverishly, he felt around the edge of
the domed surface. The joint with the inflated tube had
been sealed with some rubbery substance. He tried to scrape
it away with his nails, but it was too tough. He felt all over
the surface. There were no holes or cracks. There wouldn't
be, of course – the thing had to be waterproof. There was
no way in. And no means of breaking in. He had no tool
but his fingers. The material was pliant, but strong. Rubber,

he thought. Nothing less than a knife would have cut through it. It was hopeless . . .

Perhaps he could let the air out. Then the dinghy would sink under the weight of the charge, and he could leave it, and the bomb would either fail to go off or explode harmlessly under water in the waste of the saltings. He felt around for the inflation nozzle, rotating the dinghy, exploring its smooth surface. His fingers closed on a protruding tube. Hope rose. Then, just as quickly, it faded. The nozzle had been sealed with the same rubbery substance as the top . . .

If only he had something with a point – then he might be able to puncture the air tube. A sharp piece of wood . . . He watched the water flowing by beside him. Bits of wood often floated up on the tide. But now there was nothing. The tide was still too low in the channel to carry flotsam off the saltings . . . He thought of the pile of stakes by the bridge, and of their sharpened ends. One of those would do the job. But could he leave the dinghy long enough to reach one? He drew a foot out of the squelching mud, leaned on the dinghy, pulled the other foot out, and slowly worked his way backwards to the water's edge. There he heaved on the boat, trying to strand it. It stuck on the mud, but only for seconds. He heaved again, with all his strength. No good . . . Directly the dinghy ceased to be buoyant, its weight made it immovable. He couldn't get it firmly enough aground to risk leaving it. While he was fetching the stake, the rising tide would float it off . . .

Perhaps it would strand more easily if it were upside down. Could he overturn it? He pushed it out into deeper water and leaned heavily on one side – but the tube only went down an inch or two. He tried lifting, but couldn't raise the boat at all. The charge inside the bomb must be immense . . .

Maybe he could moor it in some way? Loop one of its rope handles round a bit of the bridge? He began to haul it back against the stream. The distance was short, but every foot gained in the deep mud was a struggle. Once he sank to his thighs and would have stuck altogether if he hadn't had the buoyancy of the dinghy to help him out. All the time he was conscious of the clock ticking away. His minutes of calculated safety were already up. Sweating from fear and effort, he reached the bridge at last. The planks were still too high above the water to be of any use as an anchor. Holding the inflated tube with one hand, he felt for some irregularity in the supporting piles with the other. His searching fingers touched a protruding knot of wood at water level. It wasn't much of a hold – but it might just give him time to fetch a stake. He draped a loop over it and let the dinghy take the strain. As he did so, his precarious balance went. He clutched at the pile for support – and the dinghy slipped away, out of reach.

He lunged after it – but the tide was carrying it on much faster than he could move through the glutinous mud. Already it was ten yards away. With a pounding heart, he scrabbled his way up the mud wall of the channel, raced along the bank until he was well ahead of the dinghy, hurled himself down the slimy slope into the water, and caught the passing rope.

He held on, breathing hard. Now what? It was much too far to drag the dinghy back to the bridge again. He was stuck with the thing. The clock ticked inexorably on. It hammered in his head. He couldn't forget it for a second . . . If only he'd risked that gamble! He'd have made it. The garrison would all have been safe. Now, with so much time lost, it was out of the question. Yet if he stayed with the bomb, he was finished. That was a certainty . . .

He looked around wildly. He was standing close to the junction of the main channel with the big tributary creek – Smallgains. A mud bar across the entrance was gleaming in the semi-moonlight. He focused his gaze on it, straining to pick out some object that would help him. He didn't need a miracle. A piece of jagged glass was all he asked. Or an old protruding stump that he could tie up to . . . But there was nothing. The mud was bare. A smooth, shining bank, edged with froth . . .

Edged with froth! A rising line of froth! Suddenly Hugh had an idea. The tide wasn't high enough yet to start pushing its way up the rill – but it soon would be. The level of the water was only a few inches below the top of the bar. If he could deflect the dinghy into the rill, it would be carried up Smallgains on the rising tide. Away from the house . . . There was a chance – if the time bomb gave it to him . . .

With new hope stirring, he dragged the dinghy to the bar – and waited. It was the longest wait he'd ever known. He tried to close his mind to the ticking of the clock. Listening wouldn't help. Worrying wouldn't help. He was committed now. In fifteen minutes he'd either be dead or safe. He gazed across the saltings to the mill, to the lighted curtains of the sitting-room. Debbie must be there. He wondered what she was doing, what she was thinking.

The brown bubbles of the tide rose around his feet. Inch by inch he dragged the dinghy up the bar. The mud was almost covered now. The suspense was unbearable. Safety was so near . . . Suddenly the boat freed itself. It was over the mud. It drifted a few yards and stopped again, held by some obstruction. But now its course was set. It couldn't get back into the main channel. It could only go forward with the tide – up Smallgains. Hugh released it.

He had only one thought now – to put the barrier of the sea wall between himself and the bomb before it exploded. He scrambled up the mud slope in a frenzy of haste and raced for the bridge. He was almost there when his foot struck something and he stumbled. He fought to regain his balance and failed. His feet shot from under him. He knew an instant of pain as he fell – and that was all.

Chapter Six

BACK AT THE mill, Debbie had been growing more and more restive at the lack of news. Twice she had called up Trant on the intercom, seeking reassurance. Several times she had gone to the head of the stairs to listen. At eleven o'clock she climbed to the loft and looked out of each of the slit windows in turn. Not a glimmer of light showed on the saltings. By half past eleven she could bear the strain no longer. Pale and scared, she went down to the entrance hall.

Trant was pacing up and down beside his chair. At the sound of the girl's step he turned sharply. 'Debbie, you know you're not supposed to be here... Please go back upstairs.'

She seemed not to hear him. 'Hugh's been gone for nearly two hours,' she said. 'What could he possibly be doing?'

Trant paused before replying. 'Well – my guess is that he's found Leigh and that they're waiting till daylight before they return.'

'Till daylight! Why would they do that?'

'If Leigh's been hurt,' Trant said, 'they wouldn't want to risk another fall in the dark. It would be sensible to wait.'

'Well, why isn't there any sign of them? There's not a glimmer of light visible from the loft. And they've both got torches.'

'They could be lying behind the wall somewhere,' Trant said. 'Then the lights wouldn't show.'

Debbie looked at him disbelievingly. 'Wouldn't Hugh have come back and told us? He'd have known we'd be worrying.'

'He might not have wanted to leave Leigh alone,' Trant said. 'Especially if they're some way away... We don't know the circumstances, so there's no point in speculating. Mr Freeman is the man on the spot and we've got to assume he's doing the best thing possible.'

'But he may need help,' Debbie said. 'He may need some-one to help carry Leigh ... How can you be so calm?'

'If he needs that sort of help he'll have gone somewhere else for it ... To one of those farms along the wall, or to the village ... He knows we're not in a position to give it. We'll just have to leave things to him.'

'You can't wash your hands of them like that,' Debbie cried. 'Anything could happen ... For all you know, they may have run into the gang. They may be in terrible trouble.'

Trant shook his head. 'The gang would have had no interest in either of them unless the plan had been to attack us right away. And there's been no attack ... Now please go back upstairs, Debbie, and try to stop worrying.'

Debbie didn't move. 'It's not right to leave them,' she said. 'Someone ought to go and look for them.'

'You know that's impossible. Norris and I are both needed here.'

'You could telephone for more men ... Those reinforce-ments you were talking about.'

'And abandon everything?'

'Yes,' Debbie said, 'if there's no other way ... It's better than abandoning Hugh and Leigh. You can't just write them off ...'

'A commander doesn't break off a vital engagement be-cause a couple of his troops may be in a bit of trouble.'

Debbie gazed at him in consternation. 'Hugh was right – you *are* ruthless.'

'I'm in charge of a battle, Debbie. My job is to get this gang – and if it's humanly possible, I'm going to do it.'

'At any cost?'

'At almost any cost – because it's worth it. You know that. You agreed that it was the other day, when you decided to stay ... The position hasn't changed since then.'

'It's changed for me,' Debbie said.

'Because Mr Freeman's out there ...'

'Yes!'

'Well, I can understand that,' Trant said. 'All the same, I'm afraid I can't let your personal feelings influence my decision.'

There was a moment of silence. Then Debbie said, 'Superintendent, I want you to telephone for help.'

'I'm sorry . . .'

'If you don't,' she said, '*I* shall go and look for Hugh.'

'You can't do that!'

Her eyes flashed. 'Try and stop me. You're not *my* Supremo.'

'It could be suicide.'

'I'll take a chance.' She moved towards the door.

Trant followed her. 'Debbie, you can't do it. This is no time to give up. The gang may very well come tonight . . .'

'I don't *care* about the gang,' Debbie cried. 'I'm sick of it all. I'm sick of *you* . . .! I wish I'd listened to Hugh.' Her hand was on the latch. 'I mean it, Superintendent. I'll give you just one minute . . .'

'Debbie, you mustn't do it. You can't. I appeal to you. You're throwing everything away. We've got to get these men – they're a menace to everyone . . .'

Debbie opened the door.

Norris said, 'I'm afraid she's not receiving you, sir.'

Trant glared down at her. His hands were clenched. He looked as though he'd like to strike her . . . Then he turned and walked slowly to the telephone.

Chapter Seven

IT WAS THE shock of cold water lapping about him that brought Hugh back to consciousness. Slowly, he raised his head. He was lying at the edge of the channel bank with his legs in the stream. Beneath him, and all around him, were wooden stakes from the bridge. He must have rushed straight into the heap. He touched a throbbing bruise above his forehead and his fingers came away sticky with blood.

He sat up painfully and looked around. The water in the creek was bank high. Tiny rivulets were beginning to snake their way through the roots of the sea grass. Soon the saltings would be covered from wall to wall. He must have been unconscious for quite a while. He looked across to the mill. A light still showed at the sitting-room window. There was no sign of any excitement, no sound from outside. The bomb couldn't have gone off yet. He glanced apprehensively along Smallgains Rill. The moonlit water was empty. The dinghy had disappeared . . .

He struggled to his feet. He felt weak, and a bit dazed. He looked around for his lamp. It was lying just beyond the pile of stakes. He recovered it and switched it on and turned to the bridge. He must get back to the house. He took a couple of steps – and stopped . . .

The bridge was no longer there. Nothing of it remained but a few piles rising from the swirling water. The whole crazy structure had been swept away by the tide.

He stood there, uncertain what to do. The channel was wide now, and getting wider every minute. He wondered if he had the strength to swim across . . . He could go back by the other wall, round by the head of Smallgains. But that was the way the floating bomb had gone . . .

As he hesitated, lights blazed beyond the mill. The head-lamps of two cars, approaching fast along the private road. One of them had a blue light above its roof. A police car . . . Trant must have given up and called for help. The last thing Hugh would have expected . . .

He moved towards the wall. If he wasn't going to swim, he must get on higher ground. The tide was beginning to flow around his gumboots. The footbridge path was already submerged. He splashed through the grass, picking his way, watching out for concealed rills.

As he reached the wall, the saltings were lit by a brilliant burst of flame. A second later there was a noise like thunder and a shock wave that almost threw him from his feet. To the left of the mill – well to the left – a column of red dust and smoke rose high into the sky . . .

The bomb had exploded at the head of Smallgains Rill.

He gazed anxiously at the house. Its tall outline, stark in the moonlight, hadn't changed. Its lights still burned. It seemed to have escaped any major damage. But there was excitement in the forecourt. The police cars were there now. Figures were visible, moving across the headlamps of the cars, standing silhouetted up on the bank. The sound of raised voices came sharply over the water.

Hugh struggled up the wall and set off shakily towards the house. Acrid fumes caught at his throat. The red flame of the explosion was beginning to die down, but smoke and dust still filled the air. He'd have to make a detour round the place where the bomb had gone off. Through the fields . . . He glanced down at the meadow on his left. That was odd . . .! There was water where grass should have been. A wide sheet of water, spreading rapidly . . . He quickened his pace. As he approached the bend he became aware of an unfamiliar, roaring sound that grew in volume with every step. Suddenly he realized what had happened . . .

Twenty yards from the bend he was brought to a stop. The noise there was deafening, the scene in the moonlight fantastic. The bomb, exploding at the very top of Small-gains Rill, had torn a great hole in the sea wall at its weakest point – the sluice. A cataract of foaming water was pouring from the saltings through a broad and growing gap into the meadows ten feet below. The whole area between the wall and the built-up road was already a swirling lake. As Hugh watched, a mottled shape swept by him in the torrent. The carcass of a drowned Friesian . . .

Across the gap, men with lights had gathered. Hugh could see uniformed policemen among them, and a short, square figure that looked like Trant, and a taller man who was Norris. He waved his lamp, and Norris waved a torch in reply. It was the only reply possible. No voice could carry above the din of the tumbling waterfall.

He turned and set off back along the wall. The only way to the mill now was by the built-up road. He reached the boatyard, rounded the head of the great new lake, and slogged back along the road. There were cars parked there, and knots of villagers talking excitedly. Hugh pressed on, ignoring them. In a few minutes he reached the house.

The forecourt was jammed with vehicles. There was a fire engine there now, as well as the police cars. Armed men in steel helmets were standing around in a litter of broken tiles and glass. As Hugh picked his way through the rubble someone challenged him. Before he could answer, Debbie appeared out of the darkness and rushed to meet him. 'Darling!' she cried. 'Oh, darling . . . ! Are you all right?'

He opened his arms and gathered her to him and held her close.

FOUR

Chapter One

'I OUGHT TO have thought of it,' Trant said.

He was slumped back in one of the sitting-room chairs with an untouched glass of whisky by his side. Leigh's death had shocked everyone – but it had hit Trant hardest of all. His face was grey.

'I don't see how anyone could have been expected to think of a floating bomb,' Debbie said.

'I ought to have done ... I knew one of the men was an explosives expert. I knew they could get hold of as much gelignite as they wanted. I suspected that one of them was familiar with boats. All the clues were there ... I ought to have watched the tides more, and the front door less ...'

'That goes for all of us,' Hugh said.

'But I was responsible ...'

It was just after two in the morning, and the survivors of the garrison were coming to the end of a sombre session. Outside, all was quiet. Most of the police cars had left. The sightseers had gone back to the village. The water in the meadows had levelled off and the roar of the torrent had died. Peace, of a sort, had returned to the mill.

Much had been done since Hugh had told his story of Leigh, and the dinghy, and his struggle with the bomb. Trant had had the manager of the boatyard located and fetched from bed and had got descriptions of three men who'd been holidaying in the estuary with a cabin cruiser and a rubber dinghy. A police cordon had been thrown round the area, the neighbouring forces alerted, the ports warned. A stretcher party had been dispatched to look for Leigh's body as the tide fell. The River Board had been informed about the break in the wall. Trant had reported to his headquarters. For the moment, there was nothing more to be done.

Hugh said, 'At least, Superintendent, it's not a complete disaster. The gang weren't successful, either. They didn't get Debbie – and they've shown themselves. So, in a way, your trap's worked. Until today you knew nothing at all about two of them. Now you've got a line on them all. You may still catch them.'

Trant shook his head. 'I doubt it, Mr Freeman. They'd have known there'd be inquiries at the anchorage after the bomb had gone off... They must have been all set for a quick getaway.'

'We had the road blocks up pretty smartly, sir,' Norris said. 'And I shouldn't think they'd have made any move until the bomb went off.'

'Why not?'

'Well, sir, wouldn't they have wanted to make sure it had done its work? You don't necessarily kill everyone in a house by blowing it up... I'd have thought they'd have waited around somewhere, ready to go in and finish the job if they had to.'

Trant grunted. 'Maybe ... Even so, they'd have had no difficulty in slipping through the cordon in the dark. All these empty fields... Or they could have got away by water – landed up the coast somewhere. Picked up a waiting car... They'd have had their escape planned to the last detail.'

'Well, you've got their descriptions,' Hugh said.

'Descriptions won't be enough, Mr Freeman. These are experienced men. In no time at all they'll have new names, new clothes, new appearances. They'll get different haircuts, grow beards, wear glasses. They'll melt into new backgrounds – all prepared beforehand. I've known it happen so often before.'

'Then you've no hope at all of catching them?'

'I'm afraid not,' Trant said. 'It's no good deceiving ourselves – we've been outmanoeuvred and totally defeated. A policeman is dead – and the gang have got away. We've lost the battle... Not,' he added, with a touch of his old spirit, 'that it shouldn't have been fought... I've regrets – bitter regrets – but not for trying... Only for failing...' He got heavily to his feet. 'Well, there's nothing more to stay up for tonight. We might as well turn in and get a little rest...'

Hugh went into Debbie's room to get some aspirin and have his head rebandaged.

'You know,' he said, as she gently dabbed at the cut, 'I'd never have thought I'd feel sorry for Trant – but I do now. He looks really beaten.'

Debbie nodded. 'I'm sorry for him, too.'

'He's an odd mixture, isn't he...? Arrogance one minute – humility the next.'

'I suppose a policeman can be as complicated as anyone else.'

'Yes, I suppose so... By the way, what made him call up the reinforcements? I saw the cars on the road before the bomb went off.'

'That's right,' Debbie said. 'He'd already given up.'

'I'm surprised. I'd have expected him to hang on. He's a stubborn man.'

'Well, perhaps I'm a stubborn woman.'

'What do you mean?'

Debbie told him about her showdown with Trant.

There was a little silence. Then Hugh said, 'I'm glad you worried, Debbie.'

'I'm glad *you* did... I wouldn't be here, otherwise.'

'No... For a couple of bystanders, we both got in pretty deep, didn't we? I guess it proves something...' He bent and kissed her. 'Goodnight, darling.'

'Goodnight,' she said. 'Try to sleep.'

Hugh did try to sleep – but without success. There'd been too much excitement, too much danger. His body was exhausted, but his mind was active. He couldn't shut out the vivid pictures of the night – Leigh's battered head, the moment when the bomb had slipped away, the terrifying wait at the mud bar. The clock still ticked in his head. For hours he tossed and turned. Once or twice he dozed – but only to wake with a start, sweating.

He was thankful when the first grey of dawn showed at the window. He got up and looked out. The sky was clear, the morning fresh. He felt in need of air. He dressed, and put on his gumboots, and crept downstairs. There was a plain-clothes policeman on guard in the entrance hall.

'Morning, sir,' the man said.

'Good morning . . .' Hugh stopped. 'Did the stretcher party find Sergeant Leigh's body, do you know?'

'Yes, sir . . . He'd been washed up under the wall. They've taken him to the mortuary.'

'Is there any news of the gang?'

'I don't think so, sir . . . I'm afraid it looks as though they've got away.'

Hugh nodded, and let himself out. A faint smell of explosive still hung in the air. He walked slowly along the wall towards the gap. It was still barely light. Over on the road he could just make out the figures of workmen standing beside a lorry. Waiting to start the long job of repairing the wall . . .

He reached the gap and gazed around. The tide was out, the saltings were dry, the rills and the channel were empty. All the water had drained from the meadows, leaving a thick coating of mud and weed over the grass. The surface was dotted with the carcasses of dead cows. A macabre scene . . .

He looked down into the gap. There was a deep, water-filled pit where the sluice had been. The bomb must have gone off right against it. Maybe it had lodged under the concrete shelf and been held down as the water rose. That would account for the great breach in the wall . . . It had certainly made a mess. The floor of the gap was scored with deep watercourses. The familiar bend in the wall had gone. The shingly beach was buried under a layer of mud. It would be a long time before children played there again . . .

The light grew stronger. Hugh dropped down to the meadow and splashed through the grey slime to the wall beyond the gap. He was about to climb it and walk on when his eye was caught by something sticking out of the mud. He bent and pulled it up... It was a revolver!

He stared at it. What on earth was a revolver doing here...? Who would have had a revolver here – except a member of the gang...? Why had it been dropped? What had been going on...? He gazed around the expanse of mud. Suddenly his glance was caught and held by a tree out in the meadow. In its lower branches there was something dark. He ploughed through the mud and approached the tree. As he drew near it, he saw that the dark shape was the body of a man. It was hanging head down, as the tide had left it. The face was horribly disfigured.

He turned away – sickened, yet excited. If there was one body, there could be more. He walked on through the meadow in the strengthening light, looking to right and left. Presently, under the wall, he spotted another sprawled shape – and another... Two more bodies – both of them torn and blackened by the explosion of the bomb...

He walked back to the gap, and climbed the wall, and stood there, working things out. It wasn't hard to guess what had happened. The gang must have been waiting there for the bomb to shatter the mill – just as Norris had said. Waiting to rush forward and make sure Debbie was dead. Waiting at the nearest spot that would give them shelter from the blast. The spot where the bomb had detonated! Crouched behind the wall, they wouldn't have seen the dinghy lying there at the head of the rill... It was the justice of the gods.

Hugh turned towards the house. He felt an inexpressible relief that the men were dead. They'd been heartless, ruthless, less than human. For such men, death was the only answer... He quickened his pace. He must find Trant and tell him that the battle had been won after all...

Chapter Two

THAT LAST morning was a hectic one. Ambulance men arrived to gather up the shattered bodies, policemen to make a thorough search around the blast point before the tide came in, sea defence experts to confer on the damage, explosives experts to give a view on the bomb. Trant was almost continuously on the telephone, collecting information. Norris was equally busy, rushing around in the Mini. Only Hugh and Debbie had little to do. They spent an hour packing their belongings and stowing them in the back of the Vauxhall. Then they took advantage of Debbie's regained freedom and walked together into the village. Afterwards Debbie prepared a final cold meal for anyone who wanted it.

It wasn't until late in the afternoon that Trant called them to the sitting-room to give them a report on his discoveries. His manner was still subdued but his inner satisfaction was patent. The loss of Leigh had evidently become more bearable now that the enemy had been totally destroyed.

'Well,' he began, 'we've got a positive identification of one member of the gang. He had an unusual body mark which was on record at the Yard. He went by the name of Peters when we knew him. He was in Parkhurst prison until about a year ago, serving a seven-year sentence for organizing a particularly ingenious robbery in Mayfair. Last October he escaped with another man, and we lost sight of him. We think he was the brain behind the gang. He was an educated man gone wrong – clever, resourceful, and a skilful planner. It was pure bad luck for him that he got caught on the Mayfair job. Probably he was the man who represented himself so convincingly as Superintendent Jenkins on the morning of the jewel grab.'

'He sounds the type,' Debbie agreed.

'We've also got a provisional identification of a second man,' Trant said. 'If we're right, his name is Ferguson, and he was Peters' escape companion. Evidently they kept in touch. He was doing life for killing a Customs officer after a smuggling expedition – so we can take it he was the one who knew about boats. It was probably the third man who collected the photograph – and I imagine he was also the explosives expert. We don't know who he was – and he's so mutilated that we may never know. But it doesn't really matter... One thing's certain – all three of them were utterly vicious, irredeemable types, committed to preying on society. They'll none of them be missed.'

Trant paused briefly. 'Now I expect you'd like to hear something about their recent movements. Until last Sunday – the night of the fire – they were staying at a hotel in Colchester. That would have been a convenient base for their expeditions to the saltings. On the day after the fire they went to Burnham-on-Crouch and chartered a cruiser for a week's holiday. It had a rowing boat with it as part of its inventory; they bought the rubber dinghy themselves at a chandler's in Burnham. Next day they sailed the boat round here. They hired a mooring in the anchorage well away from the other boats, and after that they were rarely seen ashore. They must have taken their stores and equipment aboard at night. They had three cars between them and someone must have done a good deal of driving about, collecting the things they needed. We found three sub-machine guns on the cruiser – which is a pretty good indication they *were* intending to attack us here, before the fire made them change their plans. We also found several large containers that had held gelignite, various tools, including a saw and a spade – and an outfit for vulcanizing rubber.'

'So that was how they sealed the top of the bomb,' Hugh said.

'That's right... In addition, one of our men found a plunger this morning near the gap in the wall. It's the only bit of the bomb we've recovered so far, but it shows the type. The clockwork mechanism would have released a spring, and the plunger would have struck the detonator.

We reckon something like four hundred pounds of explosive was used – which would have made it as powerful as a medium wartime bomb.'

Hugh nodded. 'No wonder I couldn't lift the thing... How do you suppose *they* managed? They could hardly have done all that work on it while the dinghy was in the water.'

'The cruiser had a derrick for bringing their rowing boat aboard,' Trant said. 'They could have used that for lowering the dinghy when it was ready. Or they could have assembled the bomb at the edge of the channel, and floated it off on the tide.'

'Ah, yes...' Hugh pondered. 'Where do you suppose they were when I was out on the saltings? Back on their cruiser?'

'I should think so. Once they'd cleared the bridge obstruction, and started the bomb on its way, they'd have had nothing more to do. They didn't need to watch it – its round shape ensured that it wouldn't stick anywhere for long, and at that state of the tide it couldn't go anywhere except straight up the main channel... I'd guess they stayed on the cruiser until shortly before the bomb was due to go off and then crept along under the sea wall to the sluice. Probably on the landward side, where they'd have been invisible from the house windows. It would have been about the time that you were lying unconscious, so if they had happened to take a look in your direction they wouldn't have noticed you.'

'All very fortunate,' Hugh said.

'Yes – for us... Incidentally, it seems that they *were* intending to make their getaway by water. They'd left their rowing dinghy at the boatyard with an outboard motor in place and enough spare petrol to take them well out of the area. I dare say we'll be hearing soon of an unclaimed car parked at some convenient point along the coast... And that's about it.'

'So everything's tidied up,' Debbie said.

'Well, almost everything...' Trant gave Norris a slightly conspiratorial glance. 'There are just one or two more things I'd like to say... I gather you'll both be leaving today. Before you go, I'd like to thank you – and I'm sure Norris joins me in this. It may seem superfluous to thank *you*, Mr Freeman, since without you none of us would be alive – but I do, all the same... You behaved magnificently.'

A flippant remark hovered on Hugh's lips – but he didn't make it.

'And you, Debbie – you can be proud of yourself, too. You showed great courage in deciding to stay here.' Trant smiled wryly. 'Also in deciding to leave! – but we'll say no more about that... You've been a cheerful support to Norris and myself – and we shall miss you. You've looked after us splendidly.'

'In any other circumstances,' Debbie said, 'it would have been a pleasure.'

'Well, let's hope we shall meet again some time. In happier circumstances.'

Debbie looked at him in surprise. 'Shan't we be meeting at the trial?'

Trant shook his head. 'You won't be needed at the trial. Clay will probably plead guilty ... If he doesn't, he'll be convicted without you.'

'Plead guilty!' Hugh said. 'How are you going to make him do that – stretch him on the rack?'

'We shan't need to, Mr Freeman. We as good as caught him red-handed with the jewels – so he won't have much choice.'

'I don't understand,' Debbie said.

'It's quite simple, Debbie ... You see, *we've had the jewels all the time* ... When Norris and I went into the forest that night, we managed to follow Clay's tracks. They led us in the end to the spot where he'd buried the suitcase, and we dug it up and took it to the Yard.'

'Well!' Debbie exclaimed.

Hugh eyed Trant with something less than rapture. 'So that's why you were so sure about everything!'

'Yes, Mr Freeman. What you called my "slim theory" was actually based on near-certainty. As I saw it, there were two possibilities. One – the more likely one – was that Clay would be unable to give any useful directions about where he'd hidden the jewels. In that case the gang would no doubt send someone along to see if he could pick up Clay's tracks. He'd find nothing helpful, because Norris and I had been careful to obliterate the tracks and generally confuse the scene. The gang would then get straight down to the problem of tracing Debbie... If, on the other hand, Clay *were* able to direct them to a particular spot, and they went and searched, they'd still *think* he'd made a mistake, when they failed to find the jewels. In that case, too, they'd go after Debbie. Once I'd got the suitcase, I knew it didn't matter whether Clay had been able to describe the place accurately or not. I couldn't lose.'

'Yes, I see...' Hugh frowned. 'Well, you certainly led us up the garden... All that stuff about mounting a police search, tracker dogs, needles in haystacks...'

'I had to build up a convincing picture, Mr Freeman, if you were to play along with me... Actually, the forest was left wide open for the gang to take an unimpeded look round if they wished.'

'Why on earth didn't you simply tell us the truth?' Hugh said.

'I decided it wasn't necessary. If you'd refused to co-operate with me because of your doubts, I might have *had* to tell you – but you didn't... It wasn't that I didn't trust you and Debbie – but unintended slips can occur, private conversations can be overheard and reported. I've learned by experience that if you want to keep something a secret, it's better to tell *no one*... It was absolutely vital to the plan that no hint of the truth should leak out to the gang – and nothing did. I think I was justified.'

Hugh gave a dubious grunt.

'Of course,' Trant said, 'it was the fact that I already had the jewels that made it possible for me to assure Debbie that she'd be generously compensated ... It's true that the assessors didn't offer their reward until *after* the find – but if it hadn't been for you, Debbie, there wouldn't have been any find – so I haven't a doubt they'll pay something quite substantial. You'll soon have your business back on its feet.'

'My business . . .?' Debbie said. 'Good heavens, I'd almost forgotten about that.'

Chapter Three

WITH DEBBIE beside him, Hugh drove slowly away from the mill. Both of them were thoughtful, both silent. There was so much to say – and yet so little . . . They drove on for several miles. Then Hugh suddenly turned into a lay-by and pulled up.

'Where are we going?' he said.

Debbie looked at him. 'Well – I'm going to my studio, I suppose – and you're going to your cottage. What else?'

'It'll seem very odd – going off in different directions after being together so long . . . After going through so much together . . . I've sort of got used to having you around.'

'You mean you've got used to my cooking,' Debbie said.

'I've got used to your company. I don't think I'm going to like being alone in the cottage any more.'

'I dare say the studio will seem rather quiet, too,' Debbie said.

'Well, we don't have to separate . . . Do you think you could possibly live with a writer?'

'It didn't seem too bad when I tried it . . . Do you think you could live with a career girl?'

'I'm not sure I know one,' Hugh said.

Debbie smiled. 'I wouldn't bank on that.'

'We could go to the cottage together,' Hugh said. 'To-night . . . Then tomorrow we could come up to town and buy a special licence and get married. Don't you think it would be sensible?'

'Sensible?'

Hugh took her in his arms. 'I love you, Debbie – you know that. I want you with me always. I don't care what you do as long as you're around. I need you . . .'

'It's nice to be needed,' she said. 'It's a discovery I've made . . .'

Quite a long time passed before they spoke again. Then Hugh said, 'Anyway, there's a much more important reason why we should marry.'

'Could there be?'

Hugh smiled down at her. 'Of course, my love . . . I want half that reward!'

Rosemary's Baby 5/-

IRA LEVIN

The book that topped U S and British bestseller lists for months and is now a terrifying Paramount picture, starring Mia Farrow, John Cassavetes and Ralph Bellamy.

'At last I have got my wish. I am ridden by a book that plagues my mind and continues to squeeze my heart with fingers of bone. I swear that Rosemary's Baby is the most unnerving story I've read.'
KENNETH ALLSOP, EVENING NEWS

'The pay-off is so fiendish, it made me sweat. Diabolically good.'
PETER PHILLIPS, SUN

'. . . if you read this book in the dead of night, do not be surprised if you feel the urge to keep glancing behind you.'
QUEEN

'a darkly brilliant tale of modern deviltry that, like James' *Turn of the Screw*, induces the reader to believe the unbelievable. I believed it and was altogether enthralled.'
TRUMAN CAPOTE

GAVIN LYALL

'A master of tantalizing suspense'
THE BOOKMAN

SHOOTING SCRIPT 5/-

MIDNIGHT PLUS ONE 3/6

THE WRONG SIDE OF THE SKY 3/6

THE MOST DANGEROUS GAME 3/6

'Good thriller writers are born, not made.
They are one in a thousand — an Ambler,
a Fleming, a Hammond Innes —
and Gavin Lyall is unmistakably of
their company.'
JOHN O'LONDON'S

A SELECTION OF
POPULAR READING IN PAN

☐ **PRIDE AND PREJUDICE** Jane Austen   3/6
☐ **INHERITANCE** Phyllis Bentley   7/6
☐ **SHOOTING SCRIPT** Gavin Lyall   5/-
☐ **WUTHERING HEIGHTS** Emily Brontë   3/6
☐ **THE SOUND OF THUNDER** Wilbur A. Smith   6/-
☐ **ONE OF OUR SUBMARINES** Edward Young (illus.)   5/-
☐ **ROSEMARY'S BABY** Ira Levin   5/-
☐ **EAGLE DAY** Richard Collier (illus.)   6/-
☐ **THE MAN WITH THE GOLDEN GUN** Ian Fleming   3/6
☐ **THE SPY WHO LOVED ME** Ian Fleming   3/6
☐ **THE MAGUS** John Fowles   8/6
☐ **FRUIT OF THE POPPY** Robert Wilder   5/-

☐ **I CAN SEE YOU BUT YOU CAN'T SEE ME**
                                              Eugene George 5/-
☐ **THE ROOM UPSTAIRS** Monica Dickens   5/-
☐ **A SENTENCE OF LIFE** Julian Gloag   6/-
☐ **ON FORSYTE 'CHANGE** John Galsworthy   5/-
☐ **FAR FROM THE MADDING CROWD**
                                              Thomas Hardy 5/-
☐ **THE RELUCTANT WIDOW** Georgette Heyer   5/-
☐ **FREDERICA** Georgette Heyer   5/-
☐ **STRANGERS ON A TRAIN** Patricia Highsmith   5/-
☐ **STORIES MY MOTHER NEVER TOLD ME (Part I)**
                                              Alfred Hitchcock 3/6
☐ **YOUNG BESS** Margaret Irwin   5/-
☐ **THE DEEP BLUE GOOD-BYE** John D. MacDonald 3/6
☐ **THE LIFE OF IAN FLEMING**
                                              John Pearson (illus.) 7/6
☐ **SHAMELADY** James Mayo   3/6
☐ **MADONNA OF THE SEVEN HILLS** Jean Plaidy   5/-
☐ **ROUND THE BEND** Nevil Shute   5/
☐ **THE BOSTON STRANGLER** Gerold Frank   7/6

Obtainable from all booksellers and newsagents. If you
have any difficulty, please send purchase price plus 6d.
postage to PO Box 11, Falmouth, Cornwall.

I enclose a cheque/postal order for selected titles ticked
above plus 6d. per book to cover packing and postage.

NAME ....

ADDRESS ....

....